Marshal Flynn's Pilgrimage

Marshal Jedediah Flynn has resigned his office and is determined to become a church minister. While travelling to take up a place at a theological college in Illinois, however, he stumbles across a crime which he cannot ignore. It seems that before he can devote himself to the Lord's work, the marshal will be compelled to take up arms one last time.

Marshal Flynn's Pilgrimage

Simon Webb

A Black Horse Western

ROBERT HALE

Simon Webb 2019
First published in Great Britain 2019

ISBN 978-0-7198-3045-7

The Crowood Press
The Stable Block
Crowood Lane
Ramsbury
Marlborough
Wiltshire SN8 2HR

www.bhwesterns.com

Robert Hale is an imprint
of The Crowood Press

Typeset by
Derek Doyle & Associates, Shaw Heath
Printed and bound in Great Britain by
4Bind Ltd, Stevenage, SG1 2XT

CHAPTER 1

In the early summer of 1872, Marshal Jedediah Flynn, then forty-two years of age, felt an overpowering urge to give up his current line of work and to go out into the world to witness for the Lord. He had always been a God-fearing man and regular church-goer, but this was something quite different. He honestly believed that he had been born again in the Spirit. His employers were far from enchanted by this unlooked-for development and did their best to dissuade the marshal from taking any rash and irrevocable action as touching upon his future, but it was all to no avail. In May 1872, Jed Flynn was offered a place at a theological college where he would train for the ministry. Two weeks later he handed in his papers and left his job, the Deity having called him to a far higher vocation than merely the apprehension of wicked men.

His studying at the seminary in Lafayette was not scheduled to start until the beginning of September, and so Jed Flynn had the whole entire summer before him to do with as he wished. He had some savings and conceived the notion of travelling to Lafayette on foot, preaching the word of God as he went. If he covered twenty miles a day and rested on the Sabbath, then the journey should take no more than six or seven weeks. It was the time of year when sleeping in the open would be a pure pleasure and he had no doubt that some hospitality would be extended to him at churches which he might visit on his way. The more he thought over the scheme, the sounder it seemed. He decided that he would take little money with him, just enough for food. Like our Saviour, he would walk the land, telling all who would listen of the good news of God's love.

So it was that on a fine day in June a strange figure would have been seen approaching the little town of Harker's Crossing in the south of Missouri, nigh to the state of Kentucky. The man, in his middle years, sported a short, iron-grey beard and was clad soberly in black. A leather bag over his shoulder held all his worldly goods, and in his hand was a stout ash walking-staff almost as tall as he was.

Flynn felt better and healthier than he had done for years. He had walked in excess of a hundred and fifty miles in the last week and a half and had thoroughly enjoyed every step of the way. When he had set off, the former marshal had thought of this journey as a pilgrimage, but truth to tell it felt like a regular vacation. His preaching had been well enough received for the most part, and churches on the way had indeed welcomed him and offered him hot meals and beds for the night. All in all, this excursion was proving a pleasant change from his old life and a refreshing break before he settled down to his studies in Lafayette.

The terrain over which he was presently passing was not especially prepossessing, consisting of vast and seemingly limitless stretches of flat grassland, and Flynn was glad to see in the distance the town to which he was making his way. The land sloped gently down to the north, in the direction that he was travelling, and another two miles should see him there. It was coming on evening and he had walked a little over twenty-five miles that day and would be glad to rest for the night. The minister at Harker's Crossing had been particularly recommended to Flynn before he had set off on his 'pilgrimage' as being a pious and devout man.

They do say that man proposes but God disposes, and it is a fact that despite all Jedediah Flynn's most careful plans, he was not destined to go much further north in the direction of Lafayette for some considerable time. As he approached a little soddy, which was surrounded by a neat vegetable garden, a woman came hurrying out who was, by the look of her, evidently desirous of speaking to him. She was a drab-looking creature of indeterminate age who could, thought Flynn, have been anything from twenty-five to forty-five years of age. The thing that

7

drew his attention was her hands. The expression 'wringing one's hands' was familiar to him, but never before had he actually seen such a thing in real life. Just as though she were indeed wringing out a wash-cloth and squeezing the water from it, the woman grasped each hand in turn with the other and twisted and pulled at them. It was fascinating to watch. Then she spoke, in a whining and ill-educated voice.

'I'm right sorry to be troublin' of you, but would you be going into yonder town?'

'Why, yes, I am. Can I carry some message for you?'

''T'ain't that, sir. It's my Mary.'

'Your Mary?' said Flynn, unable to decide from her tone if Mary was a horse, dog or human person. 'Forgive me, I don't rightly understand you.'

'My daughter. She works in town. A-sweepin' up and suchlike in the store, you know.'

The woman stopped speaking and stared expectantly at Flynn as though this would make everything clear to him. Her way of talking, combined with the slack and vacant expression on her face, led him to suppose that perhaps she was not quite as well endowed mentally as the average member of the populace. He said gently, 'You'll have to tell me a little plainer, ma'am. What it is you would have of me?'

She seemed surprised, as though the nature of the difficulty was self-evident. Then she said slowly and carefully, as if it were Flynn who lacked any sense, 'Mary works in town. At the store. She should have been back soon after midday, but she's not. I can't think what's become of her.'

'Ah, you want that I should ask her employer when she'll finish? Of course. Which store would it be?'

'Biggest in town. Can't miss it. Could you bring her back with you? She might not come else. She ain't what you'd call sharp. 'Sides which, she's little more than a child. Just turned fifteen.'

'Where's your husband?'

'Dead.'

Flynn hesitated for a moment. The town was a good mile and a half away and fetching this wretched woman's child and then bringing her back home would add three miles walking before he could set down and relax for the night. He felt ashamed of himself and recollected that he was a disciple of Jesus and that the widow and orphan were peculiarly beloved by the Lord. 'Of course I shall. You may be sure of it.'

Slow she might have been, but the woman was not so addled in her wits that she had not noticed the pause before this stranger had agreed to her request. She said, 'You'll truly do it? On your oath?'

'I promise you I will engage to fetch your daughter and bring her home to you. I pledge my word to it.'

She seemed satisfied with this and to trust implicitly that he would fulfil this commission. 'It's right good of you to do this. I'm sure I'm thankful.'

'It's nothing. I'll be back directly.' Having said which, Jed Flynn set off at a smarter pace than he had been making when he arrived. The sooner he found this girl and took her home, the sooner he would be able to rest. Despite his intention to perform an act of Christian charity, he found himself muttering as he went, 'This is a dam . . . blessed nuisance!' He was glad that he had been able to stop himself in time, before going the whole length of the expression which he had been about to utter.

There were a number of small stores in Harker's Crossing, but the one on Main Street stood out as far and away the largest. The owner was just getting ready to put up the shutters when Flynn walked in. The man said, 'We was just closing up, you caught me in time though. What can I do for you?'

'You have a girl called Mary working here?'

'Why d'you ask, mister?'

Flynn's eyes narrowed a little. His old occupation had taught him to be a little suspicious of men who were in the habit of answering a question with a question of their own. He had observed that such individuals often seemed to have something they wished to conceal. He said mildly, 'Her mother asked me to look in and see what's become of the girl. She was expecting her home long since.'

'She left here . . . why it must be four or five hours since. When did you speak to Mrs Shanahan?'

'A half hour ago.'

The storekeeper rubbed his chin and looked a little uneasy. At length, he said slowly, 'Fact is, I'm a-feared some mischief in the case. Don't rightly know what to do about it though.'

'Her mother said that the child has just turned fifteen. Is that so?'

'I reckon so.'

'Well then, if something's become of her, you best tell me what's what.'

Spending almost the whole of your adult life as a lawman is apt to give a man a certain demeanour that can appear a little daunting to others. Certainly the man behind the counter of the store felt unaccountably that he was obliged to furnish some kind of explanation to this stranger. He said, 'Happen if you've seen her mother, then you'll guess that young Mary ain't by way of being the brightest of souls. She might have the body of a woman, but her mind's more like that of a little girl, if you take my meaning. Well then, she's been hanging round the saloon across the way, the Lucky Seven. I warned her 'bout it, but something about the place takes her fancy. Some o' the men there, they're not overly bothered about a young lady's mind, if you take my meaning. I thought she was at hazard and walked out to speak on it to her mother couple of days since.'

'What d'you think's befallen her?'

'I shouldn't wonder if some fellow hasn't taken advantage of her, who knows?'

'You think anybody in the saloon might know anything?'

'I couldn't say, I'm sure.'

'You've a sheriff round here?'

11

The man's lips thinned and he nodded. 'Don't think you'll get much help there, though.'

It was tolerably clear to Jed Flynn that he was not just going to be able to drop by the church and settle down for a pleasant evening meal with the minister and his wife. This looked like a job that would take some little time. Still and all, he had given his word to that woman and so felt a bounden duty to do all that he could in the matter. This did not precisely sweeten his temperament, and so when he strode through the batwing doors of the Lucky Seven he was in no mood to hear any pussyfooting around or prevarication.

As he walked to the bar, Flynn was unaware of what a striking figure he made with his staff. The saloon was not very crowded at that time of day and the bartender came straight over to see what this new customer's pleasure might be. Flynn said, 'I'm not here to drink. I was wondering if you knew anything about a young girl who by some accounts has been hanging around here. Maybe she's been seen outside?'

'There has been a girl standing around, peering through the doors at the folk drinking in here,' admitted the bartender, 'I've had to shoo her away a few times, she was making men uneasy.'

'When last did you see here?'

'Yesterday, I think. What's it to you? You ain't the law, I'll be bound.'

Until he had quit his job a month or so earlier, Jed

Flynn had had a very disconcerting habit when trying to acquire information. He would simply remain silent and stare at the person to whom he was talking. This invariably had the effect of making people a little nervous and liable to reveal something interesting. So it was that he now just looked at the man in front of him impassively, waiting to see what else would come to light. The man reddened slightly under this scrutiny and he began to polish a glass with a cloth. Then he said in a low voice, 'Don't look round now, but there's three men sitting at a table over at the back there who might be able to help you. They've some connection with a hurdy house, if you know what that is.' Then he announced loudly enough for all to hear, 'Sorry I ain't able to help you further, mister.'

Flynn nodded and then went around the place, asking if anybody knew of the girl Mary's whereabouts. He was careful to leave until last the table where sat three villainous-looking and ill-favoured characters whom he would at once have known were up to no good, even without the hint from the bartender. They had that indefinable air about them of men who were separate from ordinary society.

'I wonder if you fellows might help me,' said Flynn pleasantly, when he reached their table. 'I'm trying to find a girl called Mary. She's just fifteen years of age and by all accounts was frequenting the front of this establishment till lately.'

'You the law?' growled one of the men, 'Don't see

a badge.'

'Don't you trouble your head about that,' said Flynn evenly, 'just answer my question.'

The man to whom he was speaking got to his feet and said, 'I don't take overmuch to men who ask questions of me.'

There was a hush, as all conversations in the barroom tailed off and every eye was directed towards the scene unfolding at the back of the room. The man facing him was sporting not one, but two pistols, a trick that Flynn had always associated with bullies and braggarts, and men who needed a little reassurance that they were manly enough. He stared hard into the fellow's eyes and said softly, 'You don't want to get crosswise to me.'

For two or three seconds, there was dead silence and it looked as though violence might be about to erupt. The other two men who had been seated at the table rose to their feet too, but instead of falling upon Flynn, one of them said to the man facing Flynn, 'Come on, Pete. We got more important fish to fry,' whereupon all three of them walked past Flynn and left the saloon. Conversations were resumed as the patrons of the Lucky Seven saw that they were not to be entertained that evening by a display of fisticuffs or gunplay.

The mention of hurdy houses had chilled Flynn's heart and he felt that this was now perhaps a situation that he could hand over to the law. The storekeeper had been curiously unenthusiastic about

14

the prospects of the local sheriff taking an interest in the business, but he knew that he would at least have to try.

What passed for the main street of Harker's Crossing was in the main occupied by residential dwellings, interspersed with small businesses. Apart from the stores, saloon, church and livery stable, only one building stood out as not being either a store or somebody's dwelling house, and this proved to be the sheriff's office. There was a light burning within and so Jed Flynn figured that he might just as well march in and set out the facts for the sheriff to make of them what he would.

Sheriff Lacombe was a genial and seemingly good-natured man, about the same age as Flynn himself. After Flynn had introduced himself, Lacombe listened carefully to the story and then said something surprising. 'What I don't seem to get, Mister Flynn, is your interest in this. You don't even know this girl, is that right? Never even met her, from what you say.'

'I'd o' thought that a missing young girl is any citizen's business,' said Flynn, a little stiffly. Then, fearing that he had sounded a little priggish, he added, 'Besides which, I gave my word to her mother. I told her that I would bring her daughter home to her and I'm a man who does what he says he'll do.'

'That won't answer here,' said Lacombe, his face hardening. 'You take my advice: you'll leave this in my hands. I'll see what I can do, but when all's said and done, you're only a private citizen. It's really no

15

affair of yours.'

Had he but known it, Sheriff Lacombe could hardly have taken a worse tack than this, for Jed Flynn felt all his hackles rising at such a cavalier attitude to the law. He said, 'I think you'll find that you're quite mistaken there, my friend. It's right enough that I'm "only", as you phrase it, a citizen. But citizens have duties and responsibilities, just as any lawman does. A duty to prevent a felony if we see one in progress, and a duty to inform the law of certain things that we discover. I'm surprised you don't know that. In this case, a minor has disappeared and there's nobody knows what's become of her. Any citizen has a responsibility, legal and moral, to do something about that.'

'What are you, a lawyer or something?'

'No, like you say I'm just a private citizen. I can see that I shall have to stay in town for a spell and see what's become of this girl. In the meantime, I must apprise her mother of what I know. I'll wish you good evening, Sheriff Lacombe.'

As he walked back towards the little house where he had encountered the anxious mother, Flynn's irritation at being delayed in his journey north became transmuted into a certainty that something here was very wrong and he would have to deal with it himself. That sheriff had been worse than useless: he was, unless all Jed Flynn's well honed instincts were playing him false, complicit somehow in the child's disappearance. This was, to Flynn, a most shocking idea. He had come across corrupt peace officers before, of course, but on each and every occasion had felt an overwhelming sense of revulsion, as though in the presence of a loathsome reptile. It was his strong feelings on this subject that had made him so valuable in law-keeping and accounted, at least in part, for the great reluctance shown by his superiors to accept his resignation.

It was still light, although the sun was at the point of setting. The woman he had spoken to earlier was still standing outside her home and it occurred to Flynn to wonder why she had not simply gone to town herself to enquire after her daughter. This was a minor mystery to which he never found an answer. Seeing him approaching alone, the woman, who was still wringing her hands, cried out reproachfully, 'You promised! You took an oath to bring her home.'

'And so I will,' he called back. 'I need to go look for your daughter, though.'

When they were close enough to have a conversation without the need to yell, Flynn acquainted the woman with the fact that her child appeared to have left town, although nobody could be sure about this. He assured her that he would not rest until he had tracked down Mary and brought her home. The fact that he had promised to do this before weighed heavily on his mind. He was not a man to make such an undertaking lightly and although he had not known what a hard row this was likely to be when he pledged his word, he knew that he could not break faith now.

When explaining things to Mary Shanahan's mother, it had not seemed to Flynn necessary to mention what the bartender had said to him about a hurdy house perhaps being involved. There was no point worrying this poor soul to death; she looked plumb distracted as it was. Before leaving, he asked if there was anybody she could talk to or perhaps go and stay with until he brought home her child. She shook her head listlessly and so he took his leave.

There was a clear view from the Shanahans' soddy all the way down the slope to the town, and as he left the place, heading back to Harker's Crossing, Flynn saw three figures heading towards him from the town. His heart sank, because it was too much of a coincidence and he had not the slightest doubt that these were the same men whom he had lately accosted in the Lucky Seven. 'And if they mean well by me, then I'm a Dutchman!' he muttered under his breath.

Flynn met up with the men about midway between the town and the Shanahans' home. As he had suspected, these were the same three men he had run into at the saloon, and by the look on their faces their intentions towards him were anything but friendly. He received startling confirmation of this when one of them pulled a gun from its holster and drew down on him. Flynn held up his left hand pacifically, palm outwards, while retaining firm hold of the staff in his right hand. In a perfect counterfeit of timidity he backed away nervously, saying as he did so, 'Hey, I'm not looking for any trouble!'

Emboldened by this apparently fearful response, the fellow with the pistol lowered it as his two partners moved forward. This man had chaffed the others greatly after they had left the saloon, asking why anybody would have been afraid of that scarecrow with the walking staff. He had asserted warmly that at the first sign of resistance, the man would cower in fear – and so it had proved. He was then vastly surprised when Jed Flynn swung his staff down on the wrist holding the gun with sufficient force to break the bone, which shattered with an audible crack. The gun dropped from his nerveless fingers.

Having dealt with the most dangerous of his opponents, the one armed with a deadly weapon, Flynn turned his attention to the other two. He rammed the stout length of wood into the face of one, striking him in the mouth hard enough to dislodge a half-dozen of teeth and break a few more. Then he disposed of the remaining man by bringing down the wood on the top of his skull, rendering him unconscious. 'Like I say, I'm not looking for trouble,' he said, 'but if you fellows want any, I've plenty and to spare for you.'

With one man laying senseless, another with both hands clamped to his ruined mouth and the third moaning in agony and nursing a broken arm, Flynn reckoned that he could take a little time to draw their fangs a little more. He went first to the man who had accosted him at gunpoint and picked up his pistol. He then went over to the man who would never again smile without remembering the day he thought he could get the better of Jed Flynn, and reached down to extract his gun from its holster. There was no objection from the owner of the firearm. Lastly, he turned his attention to the man whom he had knocked out. This was the one with two guns who had taken exception to being questioned earlier that day. He took both his guns as well. All four of the firearms that Flynn had confiscated were of the cap and ball type. He rendered three of them harmless by tapping out the wedges that secured the barrels to the body and held the cylinders in place on their spindles. Having done so, he threw the component parts away and retained the little steel wedges. The fourth gun he popped into his bag. He might have finished with violence and killing for his own part, but that did not mean to say that he was yet prepared to offer himself up as a lamb for the slaughter. He'd a notion that getting back the poor woman's daughter might be no easy task and he'd feel better in his own mind if he had a pistol at hand.

Having ensured that none of those present posed any threat to him, Flynn said, 'I've no time to waste bandying words with you skunks. Here's how matters lay. I want to know where that child is. I've an idea you men know. Tell me all you know and I have no

further interest in you. I'll let Sheriff Lacombe deal
with you.'

The man whose wrist he had broken said,
'Lacombe! It's him as set us after you. Said as you
were dangerous and we should knock you about a
bit, get you to leave town and stop asking questions.'

'Where's the girl?'

'She's fine. We just come by little towns like this
every so often. We collect girls to work in hurdy
houses over in Kentucky. There's another gone
today.'

'How are they getting there?'

'We just kind of escort them to the road outside
town. Fellow with a carriage took 'em off. Both of
them.'

'You know how old that child was?'

The man shrugged. 'Didn't ask. She was keen
enough to go off travelling.'

'Carry on like this and you're like to get your other
arm broke,' said Flynn quietly. 'Where were they
heading?'

'Just across the state line. Place called Birkinville.'

Jed Flynn thought all this over for a space. The
man whose mouth he had smashed in was groaning
and rocking to and fro in pain. The third of them
still lay supine and Flynn wondered if perhaps he had
done him more of a mischief than he had realized.
Not that he had much sympathy for the fellow, but it
could make for complications. He said, 'You know
that trafficking in girls like this is a hanging matter in

21

some countries? You men are the lowest types, but I don't have time to waste on you. Cross my path again and things might turn out worse for you. I hope we're clear about that.'

Flynn knew then that keeping his oath and bringing back that child to her mother would be no easy matter, and most likely entail some violence along the way. He began walking back to Harker's Crossing.

CHAPTER 2

Some seventy years before Jedediah Flynn arrived in Harker's Crossing, a lot of people in the little German state of Hesse were struggling to survive. Farmers had been dividing their land up to provide an inheritance for their children until the plots were so small that they could not support the families tending to them. Some enterprising types began making brooms and other utensils to sell around the towns, but the competition was stiff and they still found it hard to make ends meet. That was when some bright soul hit upon the idea of getting his daughter to attract the attention of those passing in the street by playing the hurdy-gurdy and dancing. Hurdy-gurdys are hand organs, consisting of a rosined wheel that is turned by a handle and rubs against a set of strings. Chords are then played by operating keys.

Attractive young girls dancing to music certainly brought a crowd flocking and some of those who watched then went on to buy the wares on offer. The notion spread throughout that part of Germany and when some of these folks later emigrated to the United States, they brought with them their hurdy-gurdy. In time, the selling of the fly whisks and brooms was abandoned and the dancing and playing were all that was undertaken, there being no shortage of men who would cheerfully pay to see a girl of seventeen or eighteen dancing to the strain of a hurdy-gurdy.

Within a few years of the arrival of the first hurdy-gurdy girls, houses began to be set up where the entertainment could take place in more comfortable surroundings than a windy street corner. These became a cross between saloons and theatres and were tremendously popular with lonely men who didn't get much female company. Inevitably, some of the girls went on to greater intimacy with the customers than merely singing and playing in front of them on a stage, and by the time that the War Between the States racked the nation, hurdy houses had become more or less synonymous with low life and, all too often, prostitution. So many of the young women playing their hurdy-gurdy got into the way of being what were known as 'upstairs girls', that the very expression 'hurdy girl' came to suggest a young woman of easy virtue. All of this was tolerably familiar to Jed Flynn and accounted for his perturbation of mind as he hastened back to Harker's Crossing that fine June evening.

Knocking about those three scallywags had left Flynn feeling faintly disgusted at himself. Whatever had become of his avowed aim of turning the other cheek, as our Lord advocated? This was a fine way to carry on for a man who hoped to become a minister! Mind, set against that was the fact that a fatherless child was probably in peril and the sooner he tracked her down and rescued her, the better it would be. Perhaps a few bumps and bruises inflicted upon those worthless individuals was just straw in the wind compared to the saving of a young girl. But then again, that was a dangerous road to take: arguing that the end justified the means.

It was while brooding in this discontented fashion that Flynn suddenly discovered that he was ravenously hungry and then, hot on the heels of this realization, came the remembrance that he had been promised a hearty welcome at the home of the minister of Harker's Crossing's Baptist church. This struck Flynn as a happy coincidence and he delved into his bag for the list of names and addresses that he had been given before he set out on his pilgrimage: people who would provide him with shelter and sustenance on his journey to Lafayette.

The Reverend Michael Phipps and his wife were delighted to welcome Flynn into their home. They were just preparing for their evening meal and so he had timed his arrival well. It was taken for granted that he would be offered a bed for the night and so they showed him up to the room where he would be staying and gave him the chance to freshen up a little.

To begin with, the meal was a pleasant change from recent experiences. It was nice to set down at a table and eat like a civilised being and the Phipps were good company. They asked Flynn if he would like to say grace, which he did. It was when the conversation drifted to the state of morals in the town and surrounding country that things took an ugly turn.

'Speaking in general,' said Reverend Phipps, 'our young folk hereabouts are decent and God-fearing. Mind,' he continued, turning to his wife, 'We get the exceptions to the rule, don't we, dear?'

'I'm afraid so.' Mrs Phipps looked sad to be considering the depravity of a small section of the local young men and women. 'Still, the boys often get a little encouragement to leave the district and go off to join the army or whatever they wish to do, away from this neighbourhood. As for the girls, well, they also seem to find their way to other parts where their conduct does not cause so much upset and shock as it does around here.'

Flynn was aware that some communities rid themselves of troublesome young men by persuading them to go elsewhere to sow their wild oats and run riot. Once they were ready to settle down a bit, they were usually welcomed back with no hard feelings on either side. It was the first time that he had ever heard mention of a similar process for girls, though.

He asked curiously, 'I know how boys can be roughed up a little by irate family men and urged to leave town for a few years . . . when they've been making a nuisance of themselves, that is. What happens though with the girls? That's something I never heard of before.'

Both the Phipps smiled in a satisfied way and Mrs Phipps said delicately, 'The way some of those young women carry on when they reach a certain age is just plain scandalous, Mister Flynn. Just scandalous. Me and my husband have to consider the morals of everybody hereabouts. You know how one bad apple can contaminate others? It's the self-same thing with a bad girl. She has a deleterious effect upon all those around her. Leads 'em into sin.'

'You know what scripture teaches us about it?' asked the minister. 'You shall not suffer a harlot to dwell among you.'

A horrible suspicion gripped Flynn and he hoped earnestly that he was mistaken. He kept his voice studiedly neutral and replied casually, 'Yes, I'm acquainted with the text. So where do they go, these "bad" girls?'

'Why,' said Phipps, 'we let them know that their unsavoury tricks aren't wanted in Harker's Crossing, but that there're places where they can get up to whatever they please, if they're determined upon such a downwards course.'

'There's fellows who come by the town then and when,' explained Mrs Phipps. 'They offer the girls a

27

passage out of here and some take it. Suits all parties, really.'

'You mean working in hurdy houses and such?' said Flynn, scarcely able to believe what he was hearing, 'I recall hearing something of this now.'

'Well, what I say is, if they're going to go to the bad, best they do it away from here,' said Reverend Phipps, 'At least then they can't corrupt any of the innocent souls they rub shoulders with.'

Jed Flynn could hardly breathe, let alone trust himself to speak. Mrs Phipps noticed that he was breathing heavily and enquired solicitously, 'Why, what ails you Mister Flynn? I declare, you've gone quite pale!'

Fighting to control his voice, Flynn said evenly, 'I'll tell you what ails me, ma'am. That two people who represent themselves as Christians should encourage this vile trafficking in human cargo. I never heard anything so wicked in the whole course of my life. That there are terrible and degraded men who engage in this evil, I knew. That somebody who claims to be a follower of Jesus should countenance such a thing is beyond anything I could have imagined.'

Jed Flynn was not in general one for making long speeches, and when he had finished he wondered whether he would have done better to keep his own counsel. Then he observed the smug and self-satisfied expressions on the faces of the minister and his wife and knew that he had done right to speak out.

He stood up and said, 'There's a simple-minded child been lured off by those you would see as allies. Any harm as befalls her will be laid to your account at the dreadful day of judgement. You want a Bible text to follow, I'd venture to offer the one in which our Saviour warns that anybody who harms one of the little ones, then it were better for that person to have a millstone tied round his neck and be cast into the depths of the ocean. He was talking of people like you and your wife, Reverend Phipps.'

There seemed nothing more to be said and so Flynn left the room, went upstairs to the room he had been allotted, collected his bag and staff and then left the house without another word to his host and hostess. He felt sick at heart and because he was so greatly disturbed in his mind at what had been told him so casually, he did not notice the figure waiting for him in the shadows. It was twilight and the man had been standing stock-still behind a tree. As Flynn walked past, a sinewy hand shot out and grabbed his arm, just above the elbow. A husky voice said, 'I been waiting for you.'

At first, Flynn assumed quite naturally and as a matter of course that the man who had laid hands on him was one of those he had bested on the way into town, but when he turned to look, this proved not to be the case. He said, 'You want to converse with me peaceably, then you'd best take your hand from my arm.'

The man instantly released Flynn's arm and said, 'I

reckon you're the man I heard tell of. Had words in the Lucky Seven about young Mary Shanahan.'

'Happen so,' admitted Flynn, not seeing where this was tending. 'What of it?'

'Only this: that I aim for to go after those girls as have left town this day and settle with those as took them. Two can be stronger than one.'

Flynn looked closely at the man and even in the fading light could see that he was a dirt-poor farmer. He said, 'There's a bench over there. Why don't we go and set down and reason this out?'

Moses Jackson, for so the rough man was named, was by no means the most articulate fellow in the world, nor was he in possession of a great vocabulary. Teasing out the facts of the case was no easy job and even when he had the gist of the thing, Flynn felt that there were gaps in the man's story. It seemed that Jackson farmed a smallholding five miles from town, where he lived with his wife and five children. Times were hard and there was barely enough to eat. For some time, Jackson had been urging his oldest child, Abigail, to find work, either in town or on one of the neighbouring farms. There were simply too many mouths to feed.

It was at this point in his narrative that Moses Jackson grew a little vague. For some reason he had left his family and travelled over to Tennessee for three weeks. When he had returned, that very day, it was to find that Abigail's mother had encouraged her to take a position in what was supposedly a musical theatre. A man had shown up at the farm and praised the girl's beauty and assured her mother that the whole thing was a marvellous opportunity for her daughter. Like a blamed fool, to use Jackson's words, his wife had fallen for this and allowed Abigail to go off to town that morning, from where she had been escorted to some carriage and was last seen heading east.

'I reckon as theys a-takin' of her to a hurdy house, from what I heard,' opined Jackson, 'and once there, the Lord alone knows what'll happen.'

'I guess you read the matter aright, Mister Jackson,' said Flynn, after listening patiently to the man's rambling and repetitive account. 'You have a horse?'

'Got two. One for you, if you want the loan of it. Back at my place.'

This solved at a stroke one of the most vexing problems that Flynn had been wrestling with: how he could acquire a horse, short of stealing one. His meagre financial resources would not extend to such a purchase. He'd no desire really for any companion, having always preferred to work alone, but there might be some sense in having two of them work together in that way. He'd an idea that Moses Jackson might be a handy fellow to have at your side if there was to be any roughhousing. Having mulled all this over, he got to his feet and stretched out his hand, saying, 'Well, Mister Jackson, I guess you and I might be destined to be partners for a while. Least till we settled this little business.' The other man also rose and gripped Flynn's hand with his own. Jackson's hand felt as solid and gnarled as the branch of an oak tree.

Moses Jackson and his family lived in a soddy that consisted of just two rooms: one for living, cooking and eating, and the other for sleeping. Soddies, which were common enough in that part of the country, were constructed by the simple expedient of ploughing a long cable of grassy soil, which was held together by the tough and tangled roots of the grasses, and then cutting it into blocks for building. Such homes tended to be draughty and dirty, but they had the virtue of being free to construct. All that was needed was perhaps a roll of tarred paper for the roof, although many people made their roof out of turf as well.

The interior of the Jacksons' home was smoky and stinking. So powerful was the stench of unwashed bodies, that Flynn almost retched when he was ushered in after a walk lasting a good hour and a half. The only illumination was provided by a pair of lamps that burned animal fat in shallow dishes. Apparently lamp oil was in the category of luxuries as far as the Jacksons were concerned. Despite the feeble and uncertain light furnished by the primitive lamps, Flynn could not help noticing that Jackson's wife sported a large, dark bruise on the side of her face, presumably a mark of her husband's displeasure when he returned home to find that his eldest child had practically been consigned to a life of prostitution.

Because the little house was so cramped, Flynn elected to sleep under the stars, assuring Jackson, with complete truthfulness, that he preferred that to being inside. A circumstance that Flynn noted was that Moses Jackson was the least inquisitive of men. He had evidently heard that the man he sought had been seen going into the minister's house, but showed not the least curiosity about what Flynn had been doing there. Nor did he enquire as to Flynn's purpose in recovering Mary Shanahan, or indeed anything else about his new partner's past life or future intentions. It was enough for him that there would the two of them, rather than just he alone, when it came to fetching back the girls from those who had them.

Jed Flynn was pleased that he was not called upon to answer questions about himself. It had not escaped his notice that he had lasted but ten days of the pilgrimage, which was to consist of what he conceived to be a Godly life of contemplation and self-denial, before he was off chasing lawbreakers again. It was all very well to prate about turning the other cheek and proclaim solemnly that all those who took the sword would die by it, but he had broken a few bones with his staff and now had a deadly weapon concealed in his bag. Whatever else this might be, Flynn was pretty sure that it wasn't the path to righteousness!

Before he stretched himself out to sleep under an oak tree, Jedediah Flynn felt it only right and proper to explain his motives and intentions to the Deity, seeing as he had left the path upon which he had been travelling in the direction of becoming a full-time servant of the Lord. He knelt and said apologetically, 'Lord, I know I was heading up to Lafayette, but like, you know, something's come up. I know too as I swore an oath to have no more to do with guns and such, but I'm hopeful that the present circumstances will allow me to deviate somewhat from that. I'll be back on the right path soon enough though, when I've dealt with this little bit of unpleasantness. I hope you understand.'

Flynn's petition to the Almighty was met with a chilly silence, by which he understood that he was currently out of favour with the Lord. However, the thought of those girls being taken off to a life of vice helped Flynn to bear this estrangement from his maker. He knew that he would be able to patch things up and be on good terms again, just as soon as he could settle this bit of business.

The two men set off at first light, after an inadequate bowl of gruel. It looked to Flynn as though he might have to provide the money for food on the expedition, but while he was thinking this, Moses Jackson reached down an ancient fowling piece from where it was hanging on the wall and said, 'I guess I can get us some vittels as and when.'

It was a fine morning, and despite the serious

nature of their journey Flynn could not help but enjoy the feeling of the sun on his face as they rode towards the dawn. Jackson was a man of few words, which suited both parties well enough, because Flynn could not abide pointless chatter. They had gone the better part of five miles at a good trot before either spoke.

'You know Birkinville at all?' asked Flynn.

The other man grunted noncommittally. 'Been there.'

'Is there a hurdy house in the town?'

'Wouldn't know,' said Jackson. 'Not the place I'd be going.'

In addition to the musket he had slung over his back, Moses Jackson had at his hip, in an old dragoon holster, the largest pistol upon which Flynn had ever set eyes. After they had ridden another six or seven miles, he ventured to ask about this weapon. It was a happy choice of subject, for Jackson became almost lively in his response. He said, 'You never seen one? Colt Walker. Fifteen inches long and weighs four and a half pounds.'

'Four and a half pounds!' exclaimed Flynn, 'Lord a-mercy, that's the deuce of a weight.'

'Sixty grains in each chamber. Twice what you have in your weapon, I'll be bound.'

'Must kick like a mule.'

Jackson smiled, for the first time that Flynn had seen. 'It do.'

The track towards the state line was decent

enough when they struck it, and there were various furrows and grooves that suggested that carriages, carts and stages passed along fairly frequently. Flynn said, 'I heard that a carriage collected two girls near here and that's how they're conveying them to Kentucky. I'm thinking that one of them would most likely be your daughter.'

'Who telled you so?'

'One of them as was mixed up in the business.'

'You kill him?'

'No, but I gave him and his friends a little something to remember me by.'

Moses Jackson smiled again at that.

Both men were keenly aware that the carriage containing the girls in whom they were interested had an almost twenty-four hours start on them. It could not be helped; it would have been sheer madness to set out in the darkness, with all the attendant risks of their horses breaking a leg due to not seeing where they were setting their hoofs. It was a consolation that the carriage would have travelled, perforce, at a much slower rate than men on horseback, but even so they would be fortunate indeed if they reached Birkinville before the girls had been delivered and then perhaps sent off to other locations. In such a case, thought Flynn, it would be needful to persuade somebody to tell them where Mary Shanahan and Abigail Jackson might presently be found.

All of which was well and good, but without any

official standing, Flynn could come up with no convincing reason why anybody would cooperate with him and his companion. Promise or not, the more he turned the thing over in his mind, the less likely did it seem that he would really be able to lay hands on this child.

Late in the morning, they came upon a log cabin by the side of the road. It was a wayfarers' halt, somewhere that travellers could buy food and drink. It would have been unlikely that the carriage in which Jackson and Flynn had an interest could have passed this way without observation, for the owner of the place was sitting in a chair outside his home, ready and waiting to provide whatever services might be desired by weary travellers. As they drew near, he hailed them, crying out in a hearty voice, 'Welcome to you! Maybe you're hungry and thirsty? If so, this is the very spot for you.'

The two riders reined in and dismounted. The jolly old man, with a flowing white beard, simulated pleasure at their arrival, from which Flynn deduced that there had not been much traffic on the road that day and he was anxious to sell them something. Flynn said politely, 'My friend and I are seeking information rather than sustenance. A private carriage passed this way yesterday afternoon, heading towards Birkinville. We were wondering if you could describe it for us, or give an idea of what the men accompanying it might look like?'

The old man's eyes were hooded like a crow's and

he said, with considerable less good nature than he had lately been displaying, 'Couldn't say, I'm sure. Was you boys after buying something?'

It was at this point that the advantages of having Moses Jackson as a travelling companion revealed themselves. Had he been alone, Jed Flynn would most likely have spoken softly and attempted to cajole or persuade the fellow into telling him what he wished to know. Even then, like as not, he would have been fed a heap of lies. Jackson's methods were somewhat more direct, however. Without saying a word, his hand, which was about the size of a ham, shot out and grasped the old man by his throat. Then Jackson walked forward, the owner of the roadside halt's feet scrabbling to gain purchase all the while, as he was compelled to walk backwards towards his cabin. Once they had reached the rough wooden wall, Jackson slammed the man's head into it and held him there, his powerful hand squeezing the throat to such a degree that the old fellow's face began to turn scarlet.

'Gettin' enough air there, are you?' asked Jackson, 'S'up to you now. You can die or you can tell what we'd hear.'

Flynn had been so taken aback at all this that he had not yet had time to react and decide what he would do about it. By a mercy, the decision was taken out of his hands, for Moses Jackson released his grip on the other man's throat and allowed him to slump to the ground, coughing and choking in distress. It was Flynn's guess that another twenty seconds or so might truly have meant the death of the old boy. Jackson was evidently not a man to cross with impunity. He turned to Flynn and said, 'Ask him again.'

'I'll tell, curse you!' said the owner of the cantina. 'You damn near killed me. It was a fancy black carriage, with some cipher on the door, I don't mind what. Two young ladies within, they used the privy over back there. Two men: one driving, t'other riding shotgun. There, that's all.'

'What do you mean by a cipher?' asked Flynn. 'And you haven't yet said what the men looked like.'

'Just ordinary, nothing remarkable. Tallish, one dark, the other fair. The door had like a coat of arms, something fancy and foreign. I seed such one time in New Orleans, Frenchie. That's all I can say, I swear to God.'

Flynn knew, from his many years as a lawman, that this man was holding back and that he knew more than he had shared with them. He did not, however, wish to say this out loud, in case Jackson really did kill him. Instead, he contented himself with saying, 'Old gentleman like you might spend his time better thinking on the next life, 'stead of dodging like a fox in this one. You hear what I say, now?'

The old man shot him a venomous look and confirmed what Flynn had suspected about knowing more of the business than he was letting on, by replying, 'You'll be entering the next world afore me if you go chasing after those fellows, never mind 'bout my future prospects.'

After they had left, Flynn said mildly to the man riding at his side, 'You might o' killed him, you know.'

Jackson grunted and after a few seconds said, 'I killed men before. During the war, you know. You saying as you never killed a man?'

'Not without good cause.'

'Can't think of a better cause than this'un.'

An hour or so later, Jackson asked if they might stop for a bit by a broad and placid lake while he tried to find some food for them. The farmer managed to bring down a brace of ducks, which they plucked and gutted together. Jackson stowed them in his saddlebag, saying that they might do worse than roast them over an open fire if nothing else turned up.

Birkinville was a bustling town, with all the up-to-date facilities that one would expect from a modern metropolis, including a railroad depot and telegraph station. The streets were thronged with riders, carts, carriages and foot-going pedestrians. The previous year, the town had been accorded a city charter and now boasted its own police force. Flynn was at first inclined to make the station house his first port of call, but there was some sense in what Moses Jackson said when he suggested such a course of action. Jackson spat in the roadway and expressed himself forcibly on the subject. 'If'n there's a deal of money in this trade, you can bet that the police'll have their share. They'll tip off those we're huntin' for.'

'You may be right,' conceded Flynn reluctantly, having just seen good evidence of this very thing with the sheriff of Harker's Crossing. 'Why don't we ask at hotels and lodging houses first? I guess those girls will have had to stay the night here. They might even still be around. That carriage couldn't have reached here much before dusk last night.'

The two men secured their mounts to a hitching post and wandered up and down Main Street, asking at every set of premises that advertised rooms to let. Nobody appeared to recollect four girls in the company of two men seeking lodgings for the night. Enquiries about the presence of a hurdy house in the town also met with an unhelpful response. One of the hotel clerks saying, 'Used to have two here. Both closed down now. We're a respectable town, mister. You want that kind of entertainment, you'd best look elsewhere.'

This answer had the humiliating effect of making Jedediah Flynn blush like a schoolgirl. He said hastily, 'I wasn't asking on my own account.'

'Of course you weren't,' replied the clerk contemptuously, 'Enquiring on behalf of a "friend", I suppose.'

'This is no good,' said Flynn, after they had asked in a half-dozen houses. 'Either they've not seen 'em or they know about them and aren't telling.' A sudden inspiration struck him. 'Say, we could try the newspaper office. Folk there always seem to know more about what's going on than anybody else, and if there's a story for them in it you can bet they'll help us.'

The office of the *Clayton County Advertiser, Incorporating the Birkinville Agricultural Intelligencer* was on a turning running off Main Street. It had a large window, like a storefront, through which the printing press could be glimpsed. The editor, who also chanced to be the proprietor and chief journalist, was a young man of about thirty and he was only too eager to talk to them once they had explained their business. 'Hurdy houses, hey?' he said, 'Yes, I should just about say I did know something about them. You don't live hereabouts, I'm thinking? No? Well, then, you might not have seen my latest editorial on that very topic.' He scrabbled about behind his desk and then came up with a newspaper that he handed to Moses Jackson, who shrugged and said without a trace of embarrassment, 'No use to me, feller. I never got that far in my schooling.'

Flynn took the paper, which was folded over at the editorial page and began reading:

These hurdy-gurdy houses are breathing holes of hell, where customers imbibe torchlight, whiskey, and indulge in the quadrille and whirling waltz.

There was a good deal more in similarly flowery language, which he could not trouble himself to plough through. He gave the paper back to the man seated at the desk, remarking, 'I get the general notion. You're dead set against hurdy houses, is that right?'

'More than that, my friend. I have been running a most vigorous and vociferous campaign against those establishments for the last two years now. It's a big interest with the criminal class. I had my windows smashed, my nose broken, my family threatened, my livelihood jeopardised. You've no idea what it's cost me.'

All of which amounted to, Jed Flynn decided, the fact that this young man, who couldn't have been above thirty years of age, had found a hobbyhorse that generated sales of his newspaper. He didn't say this out loud though, for he felt that here was a man who could be of some help to them in tracking down the missing girls. He said, 'I don't think I had the pleasure of hearing your name, sir?'

'Jack Brady's my name. My father founded this paper and I took over, following his untimely death three years ago. Since when, I've had the good fortune to build up our circulation until we were in a position to take over our main rival, the Agricultural Intelligencer, you know.'

'I'm glad to hear it. Question is, do you know where those brought to this town end up? How much do you really know about the business?'

'I know more than anybody round here ... anybody not actually involved in the hurdy houses, that is. I'll help you all I can, but I'm afraid there's a price.'

Flynn's heart sank at this, for he had barely enough money to pay for food, let alone a bribe of some sort. He said bluntly, 'We've no money to speak of. All we hope is to find two poor young girls who have been lured away by these rogues.'

Jack Brady looked deeply shocked and offended that such a construction could have been placed on his words. He said, 'Lord, I don't want your money! The very thought. No, I'll help you all that I am able, but only on condition that I come with you on your quest.'

CHAPTER 3

Flynn was wholly at a loss to know how to reply to such a peculiar proposal. He played for time, saying, 'What would you want to come with us for, Mister Brady?'

'First off is where I hate those places and the villains who run them as much as anybody, I reckon. Next, I can take you to various locations a sight easier than I can write down instructions for you. Finally, of course,' he added with a boyish grin, 'it would give my paper a boost if I had an exclusive story like this. Desperate fathers fighting to regain their children before they are overtaken by a fate worse than death. You know the sort of stuff. I suppose that you are both fathers?

'He is,' said Flynn, indicating Moses Jackson with a jerk of his thumb, 'I ain't.'

'So what's your interest, if you don't mind my asking?'

'That's my affair,' growled Flynn, not wishing to

share his life's history with a newspaperman. 'As for your coming along of us, there's sense in the scheme and I don't object, long as my friend here is happy about it.'

Jackson shot him a look and then fixed his eyes on the editor of the *Clayton County Advertiser*. He said, 'If this fellow can set us on the path, I'll be obliged to him. But if there's killing and such, I need to know he won't lay an information against us to the law.'

'There's to be no killing,' said Flynn sharply, 'We aim only to get those children back home safely.'

'Sounds easy when you say it fast,' said Jackson, 'but I'll warrant blood'll be shed afore we're through.'

Jack Brady interrupted at this point, saying, 'I'm no friend of the police. They're all on the take here. You have my word.' He put out his slender, ink-stained hand, which Jackson encased in his own mighty paw.

Although still more than a little uneasy in his own mind about the way things were moving, Flynn saw that the newspaperman might well be the only lead they were likely to get to the current whereabouts of Mary Shanahan and Abigail Jackson. He therefore consented, at least for the time being, to go along with what had been provisionally agreed. After Brady had locked the outer door and brewed up a pot of coffee, they sat around his desk and laid their plans.

'I don't know what you fellows know about recruiting for hurdy houses,' said Brady, 'but the devil of rescuing these poor girls is that they generally don't want to go back home again.' Moses Jackson stirred, but said nothing. 'See now,' continued the newspaper editor, 'Some of these girls have grown up in conditions of abysmal poverty. Why, I know personally of girls aged twelve who have never had any real clothes in the whole of their lives! They just wear old sugar sacks with holes cut for their head and arms. Not that it matters, for they don't leave the land around their farms from one month to the next.'

Flynn felt a little uncomfortable to hear all this, for he had a shrewd suspicion that the life that Brady was describing so vividly might not be altogether unfamiliar to Moses Jackson. He remained silent, though.

'What generally happens is that some plausible scoundrel fetches up at a lonely farmhouse on some pretext and makes out to be struck dumb by the daughter of the house. Says that she's a rare beauty and so on. The end of it is that he offers her work in the theatre, says that she need only wear fine clothes and stand in the background or join the chorus. Oftentimes, he will provide some new clothes on the spot and perhaps a ticket to some destination where she will be met. Maybe though, he arranges for her to met nearby and carried away.' He looked at Jackson and said compassionately, 'Does any of this sound familiar to you, sir?'

'Tolerable so.'

'Once they have them in the hurdy house of course, it all changes. They are obliged to dance in indecently short skirts for the customers and then the majority are pressured or persuaded into becoming "upstairs girls". You know, I suppose, what the expression signifies?'

'You say that they sometimes don't want to be rescued?' asked Flynn, trying to spare Jackson's pain at hearing of the likely fate of his daughter. 'How's that?'

'Why, because they got fancy clothes, liquor, money in their pockets, admirers, company and I don't know what-all else. Compared with the lives some of them had, scraping a living on a patch of mud, I guess that being an upstairs girl compares favourably.'

Because he had been a lawman for so many years, Jed Flynn had a finely developed sense of danger and his reactions were a little faster than most ordinary citizens. Out of the corner of his eye, he saw two men halt outside the window on the street and both then pulled neckerchiefs up over the lower part of their faces. There could be no clearer or more obvious intimation that mischief was afoot. He shouted to Brady and Jackson, 'Get down!'

Even as he gave the warning and dived for cover, there was the sound of breaking glass, followed by a fusillade of gunfire. Thinking the matter over later, Flynn decided that the intention must surely have been to frighten, rather than kill anybody. It was still broad daylight outside, and if the two gunmen had really been intent upon mayhem and murder then it would have been hard for them to miss at such a range. After seven or eight shots, there was the sound of running feet and Jedediah Flynn gave thanks to his Maker that he was still in the land of the living. The aftermath of the shooting was even more shocking to Flynn than the gunfire itself had been, for as soon as the last shot had been fired and it was plain that the malefactors were making off, Moses Jackson sprang to his feet like a cat and ran to the window. He must have been drawing his monster of a pistol from its holster as he did so, because as soon as he was at the window, there came the crash of gunfire as he loosed off two shots at the men who had disrupted their conference.

Flynn also got to his feet and went over to where Jackson was standing. He said, 'You were quick off the mark.'

'Quick enough to get one of those bastards,' said Jackson, and Flynn's heart felt like a stone. He had honestly thought to accomplish this task without the spilling of blood.

'You hit him?'

'Killed him, I reckon. Less I'm greatly mistook.'

Leaving the editor of the *Clayton County Advertiser* cowering under his desk in terror, Flynn accompanied Jackson out of the office to see what the big man had wrought with his weapon. Just as he had said, he had indeed killed one of the men who had fired on them. A pool of blood was still forming beneath the prone figure of a young fellow who could be no more than twenty years of age. Jackson's ball had taken him in the back, ploughed a passage straight through his chest cavity and then exited in a welter of blood from the left-hand side. He lay now on his belly, his appallingly youthful face turned to one side with a look of surprise etched upon it. 'He's no more than a boy!' exclaimed Flynn in dismay.

'You ride with an outlaw, you die with an outlaw,' said Jackson impassively, 'He was old enough to wield a weapon. Reckon he's old enough to bide the consequence of it.'

'This is a terrible thing.' Noticing that Jackson still had the Walker in his hand, Flynn said urgently, 'Holster that weapon this second. It's open invitation for any peace officer to shoot you down if once he appears on the scene. Go on, you damned fool, do it at once. And don't say anything. Let me deal with the sheriff or police or what have you.'

By the time the first police officer arrived on the scene of the shooting, Jack Brady had joined Flynn and Jackson where they were standing by the body of the man who had attacked the newspaper office. A small crowd of onlookers had also gathered and they were casting curious glances at Jed Flynn, who seemed completely calm and collected and in control of the situation. He had warned one or two people whom he felt were getting too close to the body that they had best move back and not interfere with the scene of the death, as the authorities would be wanting to conduct an investigation in due season.

Without intending to do so, he was in fact behaving just exactly as he had been wont to do when he was still in an official capacity.

It took just fifteen minutes for the municipal police to arrive and when they did, the first thing that Jedediah Flynn told them was that he was a U.S. Marshal and would be happy to assist them in this matter. This was, of course, stretching the truth almost to breaking point, but the immediate effect was to discourage the sergeant and two constables from dragging Jackson and Flynn straight off to the jail cells at the station house. The sergeant said, 'Marshal, hey? What's your jurisdiction here?'

'None whatever,' admitted Flynn frankly, 'I'm a private citizen who has just been the victim of a murderous assault by two armed men. My friend here defended himself, as he is of course fully entitled to do.'

The sergeant wasn't entirely satisfied with this glib rendering of the case and suggested that Flynn and Jackson accompany him to the station house, pending further enquiries. 'All well and good,' he observed, 'to talk of self-defence, but this man has been shot in the back. What have you to say about that?'

'Hot pursuit. You can see the gun is still in his hand and he posed a mortal threat to innocent people. Go back to the newspaper office yonder and you can dig out the balls fired. They'll match that weapon.'

It was at this point that Jack Brady intervened, volunteering himself as a witness whose evidence was greatly germane to the question. This was by way of being a mixed blessing, however, for it seemed that the sergeant knew and disliked the journalist. He said, 'Why, if it isn't Mister Brady. You've a way of popping up whenever there's trouble in the wind. Going to accuse us of taking bribes again, are you?'

At the station house, statements were taken from all three men and these tallied with both the bullet holes scattered liberally around the newspaper offices and also the evidence of passers-by. The police realized at once that Jed Flynn knew the law inside out and back to front, perhaps even better than they did themselves. This caused them to treat him with a certain degree of respect. Flynn was a little anxious to know how his old employers would react to the enquiry that the Birkinville police sent by telegraph, checking his *bone fides*. He need not have worried.

Flynn, Jackson and Brady had not been locked in the cells while the investigation into the shooting was conducted. The police might not have been overly keen on the editor of the local newspaper, but they recognized him as an honest and reliable witness and had no reason to suppose that he was lying about the events that he had been a part of. In the same way, it was apparent that Flynn was, in a manner of speaking, one of their own, and nobody really doubted that he was just exactly who he represented himself to be.

A couple of hours after they had been escorted to the station house, the sergeant told them that they were all free to go. 'We checked with your boss,' he told Flynn. 'Says you're on "leave of absence", whatever that means. Still, seems you are who you say. All of you can go. Even you, Brady.'

Jed Flynn was exceedingly annoyed by the answer that his former superiors had returned to the enquiry about him. 'Leave of absence', indeed! This could only mean that they had not taken seriously his resignation and confidently expected to see him back in his post. Well, they would just see! Then he remembered that he was currently pursuing almost precisely the same kind of activity as he would have done had he actually still been a U.S. Marshal, which was a sobering reflection.

As they walked down main street after leaving the station house, Moses Jackson remarked, with a sidelong glance at Flynn, 'Marshal, hey? You kept that quiet.'

'Truth is, I've left my job now,' explained Flynn. 'I shouldn't have told them I was a marshal, it's not really true.'

'If you say so,' agreed Jackson easily, 'but it surely smoothed our path a little back there.'

Jack Brady said, 'If you boys will agree to have me as your guide, I can start asking at once about those girls you seek. Give me some description of them.'

Jackson sketched a word-picture of his daughter and then Brady looked expectantly to Jed Flynn, who was forced to admit that he had never set eyes upon the girl he was hoping to reclaim. 'It's by way of being a long story,' he said, 'but I couldn't say anything about her appearance. 'Fortunately, Jackson was able to step in at this point, as he was familiar with the child.

'We'll go by the depot,' said Brady, 'but you two had best wait outside. I have a contact there who provides me with information then and when. I don't want him spooked by seeing me in company with a US marshal though.'

'Like I told you, I ain't a marshal now.'

Brady shot him an inscrutable look. Like Jackson, it was obvious that he viewed Flynn as a federal marshal who was eager to disguise the fact that he was working on some case. He said, 'I'd wager a million dollars that before you two fetched up in my office, you've been asking a heap of questions round the town about girls, abduction, hurdy houses and I don't know what all else. Am I right?'

'Pretty much,' replied Flynn. 'How'd you know?'

'The shooting lately was a clue,' said Brady dryly. 'I had trouble before like it and you two arriving just as somebody fired on me suggests that you been stirring up a hornets' nest.'

Birkinville's railroad depot was a busy, noisy and smoky place. Jackson and Flynn stood outside, while Brady sought out the man with whom he wished to communicate. While they were standing there, Jackson said, 'I wouldn't have you think as I'm not grateful for what you did back there. Shooting a man in the back, that can be a hanging matter. You saved me and I owe you a debt.'

'You don't owe me a thing,' said Flynn irritably, 'Or if you do, then you can repay me by not killing anybody else while we're together.'

'I won't,' said the other. 'Not 'less it's needful.'

Jed Flynn understood very well that Jackson had it in mind to kill any and all of the men who had lured his daughter to the hurdy house, but there was little enough to be done about this for now. He just hoped that he would be able to prevent some species of wholesale massacre when the time came. Moses Jackson might be a good man to have at your side in a tight corner, but he looked to be a positive liability when something more delicate and peaceful was being undertaken.

Brady returned with a beaming face. He said, 'It's just as I thought. Four girls left early this morning, heading east. Fellow said that two of them fitted the descriptions given. They were all in fine fettle, seemingly, laughing and chattering like a bunch of schoolgirls from what I can ascertain.'

'Meaning that they might not be so keen to be rescued, I guess,' said Flynn thoughtfully.

'This is just talk,' Jackson added. 'Willing or no, I'll fetch that child o' mine back home. See if I don't.'

The next train to the town of Larkspur was due to leave in just five and twenty minutes, and so the three men purchased tickets and food for the journey, which would take three hours or so. Moses Jackson lodged his two horses at a livery stable, directing that the bill was to be settled by the newspaper editor in due season. It was while Jackson was gone that Flynn decided that toting an ash staff was an affectation which he could no longer maintain, at least for the duration of this little escapade. He accordingly abandoned it in a corner of the depot, but not without some wistfulness, for the length of wood seemed to sum up his new life and it almost looked as though he were now making a conscious effort to rid himself of the outward trappings of the new person whom he had become.

In later life, Jedediah Flynn was prone to compare himself during that trip to the theological college at Lafayette as being a little like the Canaanite general Sisera, whose story is related in the Book of Judges. It says there that 'the stars in their courses fought against Sisera', and that is just how Flynn felt about his efforts to escape his career in law enforcement. Having settled onto the railroad train with two men and determined to undertake an act of dubious legality – that is to say taking two girls who might very well have to be dragged off against their will back to their own homes – Flynn thought that he was so far from being a lawman as to be almost on the other side of the line that separates the law-abiding from

56

the outlaw. In short, he was prepared to ride a coach and horses through the law if the end result were to prove the right one for two vulnerable and flighty young girls.

Nobody was more surprised than he, when not an hour into that railroad trip, he found himself once again playing the part of lawman. This is what happened: whenever people talk of 'train robberies' in the Old West, they usually have in mind a gang of desperados on horseback who halt the train and then steal bullion or something like that. In truth, such crimes were rare. Much commoner were those who bought tickets and boarded trains like any other respectable passengers and then, once the train was in some out-of-the-way location, it would be halted by the simple expedient of one of the robbers making his way to the cab and offering to shoot the driver should he not apply the brakes. Passengers would then be relieved of billfolds, watches, jewellery and so on, and the gang would make their escape on horses that a confederate would have waiting for them at the prearranged spot where this rapine was accomplished.

The proceeds of such robberies were not vast, but it was safe and steady work. The only real hazard was some bright fellow deciding that he would tackle the bandits. For this reason, the men undertaking crimes of this kind were well armed and utterly ruthless. Flynn was reminded of this fashionable type of banditry when they had taken their seats and Jack Brady was examining his pasteboard ticket with an air of perplexity. He said, 'Say, this has already been punched a dozen times before the conductor has come near or by us. That's odd.'

Flynn chuckled and said, 'It's the latest dodge by the railroads. They call it a punch photograph.'

'Photograph? How's that?'

'When you buy your ticket, the clerk takes a look at you and then presses a few little levers, which push holes through your ticket and a duplicate, which stays in the office. Hole on one side means man or woman, tall or short, clean-shaven or bearded, dark or fair. That kind of thing.'

'What the deuce do they do that for?'

'If you rob this train and vanish, how will they know what you look like to put in the wanted poster? Eyewitnesses get flustered and give all sorts of crazy details when they're scared or excited. This way, you rob the train then all the company need do is collect everybody's tickets and match them up to their records. Yours won't be there, so they consult the punch photograph record the clerk made and that's it, a good, cool description of what you look like.'

'Well I'll be damned,' said the editor of the *Birkinville Advertiser*. 'How come I never heard about this before?'

'It's a new thing. The railroads are just trying it out this summer.'

Almost as though they had been in a play, their conversation about train robberies was at this point interrupted by the application of the train's brakes. This was done not in the smooth and gentle way that was typically done when the train pulled into a depot, but with alarming suddenness, as though an emergency had arisen. 'Hallo!' exclaimed Brady uneasily, 'What's afoot?'

'I could hazard a guess,' replied Jed Flynn, 'but I hope to goodness I'm wrong.'

That Jed Flynn was far from being mistaken in his guess was soon evinced by a commotion that could be heard in the car in front of them. The windows of the carriage in which Brady, Jackson and Flynn sat were open and they could hear screams and angry shouts ahead clearly. 'Think it's a hold-up?' asked Brady.

'Sure to be,' replied Flynn. 'Best we can do is let them get on with it and not mix ourselves up in things.' This idea seemed to suit his two companions, for they nodded and gave grunts of assent. It was, alas, not to be.

The door at the end of their car flew open and a rough-looking fellow who could not have been much above twenty-one or twenty-two years of age burst through it with a string of oaths. Flynn did not suppose that the young man was genuinely angry, but shouting profanities and threats in this way helped create a mood of compliance among those whom he hoped to rob. Combined with the pistol that he was waving around wildly, the intention was to throw the passengers into a state of apprehension that they were all about to be murdered.

'Just stay calm and sit tight,' advised Flynn to the others. 'Worst that'll happen is that we'll lose a little cash.'

In the event, Flynn found himself wholly unable to follow his own wise and good counsel, because the young ruffian began a violent altercation with an elderly woman whose earbobs he demanded. She demurred with more spirit than many a woman a quarter of her age would have shown. 'Give you my jewellery? Don't think it for a moment, you young scoundrel. Why don't you go out and get a job, like respectable folk do?'

Despite the tension in the car and the danger in which they found themselves, one or two people chuckled out loud at this sally, thinking it mighty close to the mark. The woman's reproach, though, had the effect of infuriating the man and he made a grab at the earbobs. The old woman jerked her head out of his reach and then produced a walking cane from somewhere and rapped him smartly on the knuckles with it, saying, 'Get along with you. You ought to take shame at behaving so with somebody old enough to be your grandma!'

Far from taking the hint and feeling ashamed of himself, the robber swung the barrel of his pistol into the side of the woman's head, cutting it open. It was at this point that Jed Flynn knew that he could not sit quietly and allow such an outrage to be committed in his presence. The man had his back to Flynn who, having removed the Colt navy from his bag, cocked it and stood up. Had they been out in the open and no innocent passers-by in the vicinity, he might just possibly have aimed to bring down his man with a shot to his legs, but with the car so crowded and full of passengers, he dared not run the risk of missing and the ball flying the Lord knew where. He therefore crooked his left arm and rested his right wrist upon the forearm to steady his aim. Having done this, he fired once at the fellow's back.

The ball took the man smack-bang between his shoulder blades and he pitched forward, sprawling in the aisle. Flynn walked briskly forward and, seeing that the prone figure still had the pistol in his hand, kicked sharply at it, sending the gun skittering across the floor. The man he had shot was groaning in pain and making as though he would rise, but Flynn squatted down and said quietly, 'You stay right where you are, feller. I don't want to have occasion to shoot you again.'

'I can't feel my legs. You shot me good.'

'Says in the Bible, "Whosoever rolleth a stone, it shall return upon him." I wouldn't o' shot you if you hadn't struck that lady.'

'I'm dyin', ain't I?' asked the man, with a puzzled look upon his face.

'I'm no sawbones, but I'd say it's likely. I'm sorry.'

'Hell, it's nothing.'

And so with strong language on his lips at the last, the robber closed his eyes and appeared to fall asleep. He was though, Flynn thought, still breathing shallowly. He got up and went to the old woman. 'How are you feeling, ma'am?'

'I'll do well enough. Did you kill him?'

'All but. I don't think he's long for this world.'

'Well, good riddance, say I!'

Flynn did not like to hear such words spoken in the presence of death, so turned and went back to his seat.

'Tell me, Marshal,' said Jack Brady, 'did you always seem to attract violence and mayhem in this way, or is it only since you became a lawman? I mean was it the same when you were a child?'

Jedediah Flynn eyed the speaker coldly and said, 'First off is where I am no longer a marshal, so you need not address me as such. Second, you had best not be planning to write anything about me for that newspaper of yours, or me and you are like to fall out.'

Brady, who had in fact precisely this in mind, had the grace to flush slightly and said hastily, 'No, of course not, sir. Just as you say.'

CHAPTER 4

As far as Flynn was concerned, he had prevented a helpless old woman from being brutally assaulted and perhaps even killed. His conscience was clear, and although he regretted having to open fire as he had done, that was just the way things were sometimes. There was, however, to be a sequel to the shooting, which he found so distasteful that he once again felt obliged to intervene.

There had been three men involved in the robbery of the railroad train: the one who was holding the driver at gunpoint in the cab of the locomotive, and two others whose role was to loot the passengers of anything worth stealing. One of these two men had been killed by Jed Flynn, of course. The other met a similar fate, although not dying cleanly through a bullet wound. The two bandits had started from opposite ends of the train, aiming to work their way to the centre, meet there and then leave on the horses which they had brought to the spot earlier.

63

The man in the cab had travelled like a normal passenger and then clambered over the tender to bring the train to a halt at the prearranged location.

Barely a minute after resuming his seat, there was a commotion at the rear of the coach and a group of angry-looking young men came through the connecting door from the next coach. Two of them held pistols and one shouted, 'Any more of 'em here?' Catching sight of the man who Flynn had shot, he gave a whoop as though out hunting and the others surged forward towards the corpse. Once they reached it, they began kicking it and spitting on it. This was more than Flynn was prepared to see and he stood up and walked slowly towards them, saying in a determined tone, 'That'll be just about enough of that.'

'Who're you, mister?' asked one of the men threateningly.

'I'm the man who killed this fellow and I'm telling you boys to leave his corpse alone.'

There was no telling how things might have gone, had one of the group not spied from the window a figure standing outside the coach and peering uncertainly within. 'That's another of 'em!' went up the cry and they all rushed towards the exit at the end of the coach.

Realizing perhaps that the whole enterprise had miscarried, the man outside the train turned and sprinted towards three horses, which were grazing peacefully near at hand. He vaulted onto one of these without breaking pace and galloped away furiously. By this time, the first of the mob who had invaded Flynn's coach had reached the fresh air and sent a few desultory shots towards the departing robber.

What had passed, as the former marshal later ascertained, was that the man in the coach towards the rear of the train had been set upon by some especially irritable and muscular passengers and, when once he had been disarmed, had been beaten to death. There had been just a few too many robberies of this type in recent months, and while the railroad companies toyed with their 'punch photographs' and were even hiring Pinkerton men to ride shotgun on some lines, ordinary people had had enough, and sometimes, as in the above instance, showed their disapprobation in no uncertain way.

The two corpses of the erstwhile and unsuccessful bandits were stowed in the luggage van and the train continued on its way. A circumstance which Flynn noted, and of which he heartily disapproved, was that neither then nor later was he called upon to give any account or justification for the killing of the young robber. The other passengers seemed only relieved that the threat had been dealt with so neatly and expeditiously, and nobody went to the bother of finding out Flynn's address or requiring him to advance any explanation of his actions. The bandits were dead and that was an end to the matter. He would have been even more aghast had he known that when the railroad train reached its ultimate destination, the two corpses were thrown out of the luggage van and then displayed in the depot for a couple of days with pasteboard signs affixed to them, bearing the inscription 'BANDITS'.

Jed Flynn felt a little sad at what had happened and was inclined to sit quietly with his own thoughts. Moses Jackson also gave no sign of wishing to talk, but the editor of Birkinville's newspaper had other ideas. He said, 'Before we reach Larkspur, I guess I ought to fill you two in on what to expect. It's a lively place, and if you tread on the wrong toes then matters are like to get ugly.'

There was sense in this and so Flynn indicated, without speaking, that he was listening. Brady said, 'Different towns are centred round varying economic factors. There's cow towns, towns where everybody works in foundries and manufactories, and others where they deal not in articles to buy and sell, but what you might term services. Larkspur's one such, there're others.'

'What d'you mean, "services"?' asked Flynn.

'There's more and more places since the war ended that want to do away with prostitution and drunkenness. I know some towns where saloons have been regulated to an inch of their lives, and even in Birkinville hurdy houses and cathouses have all been closed down. I doubt any of this is news to you, Marshal.'

'Like I say, I'm no marshal, but yes, I apprehend

your meaning well enough.'

'Well you can't stop men whoring and drinking or gambling for high stakes at cards or roulette, not if they're determined to do it. You can stop it happening in your neck of the woods, but all that means is they'll go elsewhere for those pleasures.'

Jed Flynn found his mood of melancholy dissipating, for the topic under discussion was one that interested him greatly. He said, 'Go on.'

'There are three towns that are within striking distance of Birkinville, which were tiny hamlets at the end of the war. They've grown because men have set up drinking dens there, cathouses, gambling spots and all manner of other things to tempt foolish men with more money than sense. Those places have grown big and rich simply by catering for the baser tastes, and they offer services that a number of cities and towns in this part of the country have lately been frowning on and trying to drive out of their districts.'

'I mind I've heard of such places,' said Flynn, 'not that I ever had occasion to visit one. Not many folk there ever call on the law.'

'That's a fact. They say some of those towns have higher murder rates than the whole of New York City.'

'That's like enough true. And it's to somewhere like that that these girls have been taken, hey? Well, this ain't going to be easy.'

Moses Jackson had listened to all this without saying anything. Now, he said to Flynn, 'You're not minded to back out, I hope?'

'Not a bit of it. But it means that if we don't set a careful watch on our actions, we could end up being killed very quickly. I'll thank you to hold your temper once we reach there and not do anything to provoke.'

Jackson didn't seem especially perturbed at this plain talking, merely nodding and saying amiably, 'Just as you say, Marshal.'

Jedediah Flynn had despaired of persuading his companions not to think of him as a lawman, but was not about to have his very life jeopardised in that way. He said, 'I'll thank the pair of you not to use any language which might leave somebody in the town where we're heading to thinking that I've come to spy on them or something. Just use my name, never mind about "Marshal".'

The town of Larkspur had grown in the seven years since the end of the War Between the States, from a huddle of perhaps two-dozen dwellings to a bustling town in which, at any one time, one might find more than twelve hundred people. Not all of them lived there, of course. Most of those whom one encountered in Larkspur were just visiting for longer or shorter periods of time. Some men came to spend a single night with an 'upstairs girl', while there were also parties of travellers who came to spend a week or more sampling the many and varied delights of the town. Whatever your taste ran to in matters of the venial, Larkspur was sure to satisfy. Mostly though, the attraction of the town lay in prostitution and gambling, pleasures which were being regulated almost out of existence in some cities.

When the train had disgorged twenty or so men and continued on its way, Flynn and the others stood around at the depot, a little unsure of how best to proceed. 'Well,' said the former marshal to Brady, 'I'll own that we might not have come so far in our quest without your advice and assistance. What do you recommend now?'

'In the first instance,' replied Brady, 'I'd suggest that we don't stand still, looking aimless. Folk are likely to pester us else.'

Brady had hardly finished offering this advice, when a disreputable-looking old man sidled up to them and said, 'Lookin' for a place to stay? Maybe you're after a girl? I can help with all your needs!'

Flynn was tempted to say a few sharp words, but this too might have drawn unwelcome attention to them and so he limited himself to saying, 'Thank you, but we are already adequately provided for on both counts.'

The old fellow spat on the ground and said, 'Ain't we the well-spoken one! Pardon me, I'm sure.' He wandered off to solicit custom elsewhere.

Feeling that they might become the object of further remark should they simply linger by the side of the tracks in this fashion, the three men wandered off towards the centre of the town.

Everywhere there were garish painted signs offering all manner of delights for those desirous of throwing their money about. The Girl of the Period saloon vied for custom with the Aces and Eights gambling hall. Both establishments were competing with the musical theatre across the street, which promised dancers and waitresses in 'short clothes'. Brady said, 'That place is one of the hurdy houses. There's a couple of others. That's not the worst of them. Least there the girls have a choice in whether or not they go upstairs with the patrons.'

'I'm surprised,' said Flynn, 'that there's been violence connected with this business, first in Harker's Crossing and then again in Birkinville. I can see that some of those running businesses here might be a little edgy if they feel their livelihood being threatened, but I don't quite see why somebody a hundred miles away would want to be beating up on a man or shooting him over what happens here.'

'What you have to appreciate is that this is big business. The amount of cash that changes hands here is beyond all comprehension. Money's the best motive imaginable for murder, wouldn't you say? Then again, there's a high turnover here of girls. Some come and then leave after a few days. You need to be recruiting a steady stream of them just to keep things ticking over here. Anything like to queer that pitch will drive some of those concerned into shedding blood.'

'While you two are gossiping like women,' interrupted Moses Jackson, 'my daughter is in danger.'

Flynn felt suddenly ashamed of himself for treating the trip with such professional detachment. He turned to Jackson and apologised, saying, 'You're in the right, of course. Forgive me; I forget sometimes that I'm done with all that. Maybe Mister Brady here could show us where the other hurdy houses are, and we could have a look inside them.'

The first of the houses that the trio entered was like nowhere that Flynn had ever been before, and he was a man who prided himself on having a pretty wide experience of life. It was, at first sight, a little like a theatre, except that rather than rows of plush seats there were tables and chairs. The other singular feature of the place was that there existed no clear demarcation between spectators and stage. In any case, the stage was only a foot or so in height, low enough that dancers could step down off it without any trouble. The supposed entertainment, the dancing and playing of a hurdy-gurdy, was pitifully awful, even by Flynn's not very musically developed standards. The hurdy-gurdy sounded to him like a cat being strangled, and the dancing consisted merely a line of girls, none of whom looked to be above eighteen years of age and some a good deal younger than that, shuffling listlessly from side to side. All wore indecently brief and skimpy skirts that ended above their knees.

The real attraction of the hurdy house was the spurious intimacy that was possible when the girls circulated among the onlookers. They cadged drinks, which were hugely overpriced, and openly solicited tips, being prepared to sit on the laps of the men in order to encourage them to part with their money. Flynn suspected that some of them would not be above picking the pockets of drunken men, if this could be done neatly and without any risk of discovery. He said to Jackson, 'I'm guessing that you haven't yet seen either Mary Shanahan or your daughter?'

Jackson did not at first answer, and when he did his voice was strained. He said, 'I'd soon see that girl of mine a-layin' in her grave than to have this befall her.'

'Don't talk so,' said Flynn sharply. 'It'll come out all right, you'll see.'

When they had left the house, it suddenly struck Flynn that nobody had raised any kind of objection to the carrying of firearms in town. Moses Jackson not only had that enormous pistol of his hanging from his hip, but he was also carrying the scattergun. There were towns where going around heavily armed was discouraged. Even where this was not the case, many saloons and places of entertainment had their own individual regulations on the matter, and carting about a shotgun in a musical theatre would have been forbidden in most of the houses to which Flynn had been. Still, there it was.

It was a fair guess, but by no means a certainty, that the girls for whom they were seeking would be found in one of the other hurdy houses. Of course, it was possible that they were being given a day or two to settle in and find their feet, but since the whole purpose of transporting them to this location was purely mercantile, Jed Flynn thought that unlikely. They would be expected to begin earning their keep and making money for those who had recruited them as soon as possible. The people running these rackets were not, after all, philanthropists. It was after the three men had left the hurdy house and were heading to the next one that misfortune struck, and it was, in a manner or speaking, Flynn's fault.

If there were one crime above all others that Marshal Jedediah Flynn had been unable to abide during his career, it was cruelty to children. His abhorrence was rooted not only in his adherence to the dictates of scripture: he also had a visceral hatred of any sort of mistreatment of the innocent and help-less. This weakness of his had been well known among his colleagues, and whenever possible they had steered suspected offences of this nature away from Flynn. This was because if he arrested some-body for injuring or otherwise harming a child, Flynn often took the opportunity to demonstrate in the most practical way imaginable just how he felt about such goings on. On one occasion, a judge had remarked unfavourably on the bruises and cuts dis-figuring the face of a man whom Flynn had brought in, accused of ravishing a little girl.

It was coming on towards evening as the three of them strolled down Larkspur's main street. Flynn had already noted that there were more children about outside than he would have thought to find in a place such as this, which appeared to have few families living in it. Although he did not find out until later, there was a simple explanation for this, and it too was based solely upon financial considerations. Employing a grown person to sweep floors, run errands and so on cost money. There were plenty of children in orphan asylums, though, whose guardians were only too happy to send them to homes where they would be cared for in exchange for helping with household chores. For those running the orphanages, every child thus placed meant one less mouth to feed. Often, these institutions failed wholly to make adequate and sufficient enquiries about the *bona fides* of those applying to have children come and live on their 'farms', and the consequence was that not a few of these unfortunates ended up lodging in saloons and even brothels, where they were expected to work very hard to earn their daily bread.

All that Jed Flynn saw that late afternoon was a little boy of no more than nine years of age, who had apparently overturned a pail of water as he was mopping the porch of a store. As he worked frantically to obliterate evidence of the mishap, a burly and unpleasant-looking individual emerged from the door and, seeing what had chanced, aimed a vicious kick at the child, which sent him sprawling off the porch and into the dusty road. 'Clumsy little bastard!' muttered the man. Then he caught sight of Jed Flynn, standing stock-still in the road, staring at him with a look of contempt. 'Something bothering you?' asked the man, in a blustering tone of voice. 'You hoping to mix yourself up in my affairs?'

'Let's leave it,' said Jake Brady quietly to Flynn. 'We don't want to fall foul of anybody in this town.'

Brady might just as well have saved his breath, because Flynn walked slowly over to the man who had kicked the child, and stepped up onto the porch with him. When he was close enough to be heard without raising his voice, he said pleasantly, 'I was just wondering if you'd care to try kicking a grown man as you did that little child, that was all. If not, then you're a damned cowardly bully and that's all I have to say on the matter.'

Nothing loath to comply with such a suggestion, the storekeeper swung his boot towards Flynn's groin, hoping to catch him by surprise. Jed Flynn, though, for all that he was a respectable and God-fearing man, knew every dirty trick in the trade when it came to fighting and roughhousing. He stepped nimbly to one side and simply grabbed the ankle that was now level with his belly and threw up his hands, all the while gripping the other man's leg. The natural result of this elegant manoeuvre was that his would-be assailant found himself toppling back and landing heavily on his posterior.

The man laying there, sprawled on his backside, did not look overly dismayed by what had happened.

A fraction of a second later, Flynn understood why this was, because he felt a mighty blow to the back of his head and then the ground seemed to tilt under his feet. He collapsed next to the man he thought he had bested. It took him a moment or two to figure out what had happened, but by that time, things had moved very rapidly and there was little to be done.

Across the street, Moses Jackson and Jake Brady watched as the drama unfolded. As Flynn strode over to confront the man who had lashed out at a child with his foot, two men holding rifles had walked out of an alley between the store and the next building. Flynn had not seen these two, being intent only on his target. Besides which, he had his back more or less to them. These two watched as Flynn and the storekeeper exchanged words, continuing to walk in that direction. As the man who had attempted to kick Flynn crashed instead to the deck, the two armed men were only a few feet from the former marshal's back. It was the work of a second for one of them to hop up quietly onto the porch and, reversing his musket, bring the butt down onto the back of Jed Flynn's head.

When he saw the man he had accompanied all the way from Birkinville being brutally assaulted in this fashion, Jake Brady made as if to cross the road and concern himself in what was happening. A hand as hard and immovable as a steel vice clamped itself on the newspaperman's upper arm and restrained him from going forward. Brady turned angrily on Moses

Jackson and asked in a low voice what in the Sam Hill he thought he was doing. Jackson replied softly, 'I've a notion those boys are the closest they got in these parts to the law. We're a goin' to try conclusions with 'em, I'd as soon do it at a time of my own choosing.' There was some sense in this and so the two of them stood still and watched what would happen next.

Although he had been a little taken aback to be knocked down without warning, Flynn was perfectly prepared to take on more than one man at a time. He made as if to rise, but one of the men toting rifles drew down on him and said, 'You stay right where you are, mister, till we's satisfied what you're about.'

The second man added, 'Just to make things crystal clear: me and my partner here are from the local vigilance committee.'

Moses Jackson said quietly to Brady, 'It's just as I suspicioned.'

In some smaller towns at that time there was no sheriff, and the only law to be found was that provided by a local 'vigilance committee'. These men, who later became known by the abbreviation of 'vigilantes', maintained law and order of a rough and ready kind. Sometimes they handed out summary punishment to offenders in the form of beatings, and even carried out hangings for especially atrocious crimes such as murder or rape. This could be all well and good when the vigilance men were motivated by a disinterested and honest desire for justice and wished to make a district safe for their families.

Sometimes, though, the vigilantes saw an opportunity for making money by charging businesses for being 'protected' from wrongdoers. In other places, and Larkspur was one of them, the vigilance committee simply looked after the interests of the rich and powerful, suppressing or driving from town anybody who threatened to challenge the status quo.

'You all right, Mister Vallance?' asked one of the men with rifles, reaching down and offering a hand to the storekeeper and helping him to his feet. 'This fellow attacked you for no reason, from what we saw of it.'

'I come out my store and he set upon me,' said the man whose name was seemingly Vallance, indignantly and untruthfully. 'He's either crazy or drunk.'

'You injured at all? Damage to your clothing or anything?'

'I been bruised and shaken, I know that much. We pay you boys to keep us safe and now see what happens!'

'What you got to say for yourself?' asked the vigilante who was covering Flynn with his rifle.

'Mind if I get up? It'll be easier to talk.'

The man watching him nodded and Jed Flynn got to his feet, rubbing the back of his head gingerly. He said, 'This scoundrel struck a child, kicked him hard. There he is, over yonder. Just ask him.'

The child referred to stood near at hand. He had been fascinated and enthralled to see his master

78

knocked down, but now that the man who had undertaken this daring act was, as far as he could see, being held at gunpoint, it was plain that his master was on top again. There was no point in infuriating the man for whom he worked and under the counter of whose store he was permitted to sleep. There were too many ways of having his life made more wretched than it already was. One of the two vigilance men said, 'Speak up, boy! Did this man assault you?'

'No sir, he's allus been as kind as can be to me.'

Jed Flynn smiled at the child, to indicate that he perfectly understood his motives and forgave him for telling such a falsehood.

'Well now, we can't have brawling in public, you know,' said the man who was still keeping Flynn covered. 'This ain't a town where such things is tolerated. I reckon we'll have to fine you.' Without taking his eyes off Flynn, the man reached down and picked up Flynn's bag. He said to his partner, 'Dave, take a look in there and see what this fellow's financial position amounts to.'

'Well, well,' exclaimed the other man gleefully, 'look at what we got here! Concealed firearm. That's another thing which we frown upon in these parts.'

Jed Flynn had been listening attentively to all that had been said, both by the vigilance men and also the storekeeper. He thought that he had a pretty good grasp of how matters stood and felt that it would be no bad thing to let these rascals know that he was under no illusions as to the true state of affairs. 'So it's a shakedown, is that the game?' he said. 'And judging by what that bullying oaf there said about paying to be kept safe, I'm guessing that you're up to the protection dodge as well.'

So fearlessly and confidently did Flynn explain his view of the case, which as it happened coincided with perfect veracity with the actual situation in the town, that for a moment the two vigilance men were lost for words. Then, one of them asked, 'You a lawman, but some chance? Or maybe a lawyer?'

'My name's Jedediah Flynn.'

The storekeeper started violently on hearing the name and stared closely into Flynn's face. Then he turned to the two vigilance men and said, 'I guess you know you got yourself a genuine federal marshal here?'

'What are you talking about?'

'This fellow. I just knowed I seen him before, or leastways his likeness. When he said his name, that's it. I 'membered.'

'Remembered what?' enquired the man who still had his musket trained upon Flynn. 'What are you talking about?'

'Marshal Flynn, here. He's been in papers often and often for catchin' folk and bringing 'em to court. Last year there was a big fuss, you might recollect. Train robbed over in the Indian Nations. Mister Flynn, here, he tracked down and killed all them as done it. All 'cept one, and he fetched him back to

civilisation to be hung. Ain't that right?' He turned
to Flynn and said, 'Speak out now, you're the self-
same fellow?'

'Yes, I guess that's so. Only thing is I'm no longer
a marshal. I'm what you might term retired from that
business.'

'The hell you are!' said one of the vigilantes contemptuously. 'You boys never give up. You're here
snooping round for some purpose. What brings you
to this here town?'

Flynn smiled. 'Just felt like a change of scenery.
You know how it is.'

'Boss'll want to know about this,' said one of the
men. 'Marshal here needs to explain what's what. All
we know, there's a crowd o' lawmen heading this way
right now.'

At this suggestion, Jed Flynn guffawed out loud
and said, 'The wicked flee where none pursueth.
Ain't that the truth! You boys spent so long being
mixed up in all manner of beastliness that you're
always expecting retribution to fall upon you. Men
like you get so you're scared of your own shadows.'

These views did not go down at all well with the
men surrounding Flynn, all three of whom scowled
angrily. The imputation of cowardice had irked them
exceedingly and not inclined them to regard their
prisoner with any more benevolence than they had
already shown towards him.

'We're goin' for to take you to the boss,' said one
of the men with rifles, 'and were I you, I'd speak

softly to him. He's got an awful short fuse.'

Jed Flynn looked coldly at the man and said, 'Well, then, that makes two of us.'

CHAPTER 5

While Jed Flynn was bandying words with his captors, Jackson and Brady stood across the road watching to see how matters might resolve themselves. When it became apparent that Flynn was being taken some-where under the threat of force, Jake Brady was all for going up and explaining that some mistake must have been made. Moses Jackson, who had had con-siderably more experience of the rough side of life, said, 'Don't think it for a moment.'

'I don't understand you, man!' said Brady force-fully. 'Aren't we supposed to be working along of him to a common end? He'd do the same for us.'

'He wouldn't, though,' replied Jackson, with perfect assurance, 'He'd do the same as we're goin' to do. He'd follow on quiet like, till he knew how the game stood.'

Since Brady was not carrying a firearm and had lived the whole of his life in respectable surroundings, he felt unable to gainsay the other, older man and contented himself with muttering, 'Well, I'm damned if I know why it's us as has to creep around quietly. We've done nothing wrong.'

The two members of the Larkspur vigilance committee walked behind Flynn, covering him all the while with their rifles. Those passing in the street affected not to see the little procession. Visitors to the town, those who had come to sample its carnal delights, had no desire to involve themselves with anything likely to draw attention to them, and those who actually lived in the town knew that any stranger who had crossed swords with the vigilance committee was more than likely to be somebody whose aims and wishes did not fully coincide with their own. In short, it was probably somebody who might be upsetting the delicate balance upon which the whole economy of Larkspur rested.

Jackson and the newspaper editor followed the group at a distance of some twenty-five yards, contriving to look as aimless and casual as could be. From Main Street, Flynn and his guards went to the outskirts of town, to a large and well-appointed house that had been tricked out like a Creole mansion in New Orleans. The property was surrounded by high, wrought iron railings, which were painted a bilious green. To Flynn's practiced eye, the aim of these six feet high spikes was as much to guard against intruders as it was decorative. By the gate hung a bell-pull. One of the men with him jerked on this, and away in the house came the sound of distant jangling.

At length, a servant came out to open the iron gate. He was immaculately dressed, but it did not escape Jed Flynn's notice that he was carrying a pistol in a holster near his armpit, which was all but hidden by his jacket. Whoever he was being taken to meet was a person who was greatly concerned about his own safety and welfare.

On the other side of the street, two men ambled by aimlessly as Jed Flynn was taken into the grand-looking house, whose gardens and grounds took up the best part of a city block. Without showing any signs that they were in the slightest bit interested in anything going on near them, the two men reached the end of the street and turned right, disappearing from view behind a stable. When they were sure that they could not be seen from the gate of the mansion, they stopped.

'Well then,' said Jack Brady, 'what now?'

'We wait,' replied his companion, 'that's all.'

'You have any ideas on how to proceed further?'

The bovine and implacable man at his side looked at Brady for a second or two, before saying finally, 'Yes, I should just about say I have one or two ideas.' And with that, the editor of Birkinville's newspaper had, at least for the time being, to be content.

The interior of the house into which Flynn was led at gunpoint was ostentatiously luxurious. The place put him in mind of a high-class brothel. Every wall seemed to boast a pier-glass, there were crimson, velvet drapes and chandeliers glittered with glass prisms. 'Somebody has a good deal more money than he has taste!' he remarked cheerfully. The room to which he was taken was even more well appointed, with heavy mahogany furniture and expensive-looking paintings lining the walls. One man remained to stand guard over him, while the other went off, presumably to find the master of the house.

After a short wait, the man who was evidently the 'boss' entered the room, and Flynn's heart sank as there was mutual recognition. The fellow was plumper and more florid than he had been when last Flynn encountered him, to say nothing of being far better dressed today, but there could be no earthly doubt that this was the same person. Michael Docherty was a flashily handsome man in his early thirties, with curly black hair, twinkling blue eyes and a mischievously boyish and disarming smile. He was also, by Flynn's reckoning, the wickedest man he had ever met.

Docherty's greeting was jovial and expansive. He said, 'Well, well, as I live and breathe . . . if it isn't Marshal Flynn. Why, it must be quite ten years since last our paths crossed.'

'Eight years, a little less.'

Michael Docherty affected a look of extravagant surprise and said, 'Really? Only eight years? Well, of course, you should know. I mean, I dare say that you keep records and so on of such things.'

Flynn said nothing, simply because there was

nothing to be said. Docherty had no reason to love him and every reason to hate him and he was not a man who would be likely to pass up a chance to repay an old injury. By the look of it, though, Docherty was keen to toy with his prisoner a little before disposing of him, as a cat will sometimes play with a mouse before biting its head off.

'But I'm forgetting my manners,' said Docherty, 'leaving you standing there like that. Do take a seat.'

Flynn chose the most comfortable-looking easy chair in the room and waited to see what would happen next. If he was going to die, and he was tolerably sure that he was, then he might as well make his last moments on earth as easy as could be.

'Will you have a drink with me, Marshal?'

'If you have some soda water or pop, that would do very nicely, thank you,' replied Flynn, matching the other for courtesy. 'By the by, I ought to let you know that I am no longer a marshal. I've no official standing at all.'

'And yet here you are, snooping round my town,' said Docherty, his good-humoured façade slipping for a moment. 'I wonder what you're up to?' Turning to on of the men who had delivered Flynn into his hands, he said, 'Get the marshal a glass of soda, will you, Dave?'

It did not escape Flynn's notice that for all the spurious bonhomie, he had been covered the whole time by a man holding a rifle pointed straight at him. Michael Docherty was carrying a pistol in a fancy rig too. It would madness for him to try and tackle these two armed men, when all he had to aid him were his boots and fists. He had little choice but to play through this game to the end and see what fate Docherty had in mind for him.

Jed Flynn had not been the first to underestimate Moses Jackson. The man might talk slowly and live in a hovel, but he was nobody's fool. During the war he had been a sapper, a role that he had undertaken with great assiduity. His specialty had been the laying of mines, which were explosive charges laid as traps for the enemy. What Jackson did not know about the handling and use of black powder was not worth a damn.

The former sapper had no particular liking or affection for Flynn and would not have been grief stricken had harm befallen him, but as he had said at the beginning of their association together, two could more readily accomplish what they hoped to achieve than one. That being so, he had determined to rescue Flynn from whoever it was that had taken him prisoner at gunpoint. And since the use of explosives was what he thoroughly understood, it was by this means that he hoped to effect his partner's escape.

Even his best friends would not have described Jackson as a subtle or devious man. Whether laying a mine or dealing with an awkward man, he was wont to use the maximum force to remove any obstacle. In the present case, this would, he gauged, mean that he would need at least ten and perhaps even fifteen pounds weight of black powder.

Jack Brady knew nothing of Jackson's plans, for that man had not vouchsafed him any information on the subject. As far as the journalist was aware, his present companion was basely deserting the man who had travelled with them to Larkspur. He felt that this behaviour was reprehensible, but had felt no inclination to share his opinion with the man walking at his side. There are some people whose shortcomings one is very quick to draw attention to. There are also others that one is not quite as ready to pull up on such things, and Moses Jackson definitely fell into this latter category. Something about the fellow warned Brady that he would be a bad one to get crosswise to.

'You got a deal in the way o' cash money?' asked Jackson suddenly. 'I don't know how much we's agoin' to need.'

'Money?' asked Brady stupidly. 'What do you mean?'

'You know what money is, I reckon,' said the other sardonically. 'Better than I do from all I am able to collect.'

'Yes, I wondered what you wanted it for.'

'Why, to get yon' marshal free, of course,' said Jackson in surprise. 'You didn't think I was such a cur as to leave him a prisoner, did you? 'Sides which, we need him.'

'Forgive me, Mister Jackson, but maybe I'm a little slow today. How will money help us? You mean to bribe somebody?'

'Bribe?' said Moses Jackson in a shocked voice. He scarcely even knew what the word meant, but it had a faintly disreputable sound to it. 'No, I ain't fixin' for to bribe anybody. I'm aimin' to blow up a couple of buildings.'

'Drink all right?' asked Michael Docherty affably. 'Not hungry at all, I suppose?'

'No, I ate on the train. But thank you for the offer.'

Docherty's two men, for so Flynn assumed them to be, were still standing guard, keeping a watchful eye upon him. Whatever game he might play of being the friendly host, these men were not deceived. They probably knew what was in store. That he would probably die this day was not as bitter a reflection as it might be for many men. Flynn knew that he had lived an honest and Godly life, and that all men eventually face a final reckoning with the Lord. If his was to come now and not in twenty years' time was just how the cards fell sometimes. Not that he proposed to go quietly. If he could at least take Docherty with him then he would be content. There was a man who contaminated the world just by his presence in it.

Docherty remarked to his men, 'This here's the fellow who cost me a year of my life. Isn't that so, Marshal?'

'It should have been more. You were given twenty

years, you know. Strikes me you got off light.'

'You call a year in the penitentiary "light", do you?'

It was, thought Flynn, at least worth trying to sow some dissent between these scoundrels. Perhaps the two men who had brought him here were not as debased as Docherty and would be horrified to know the nature of his crime. He said conversationally, 'I suppose you fellows know what it was that your boss was sent down for? White slavery. Luring wretched young girls into captivity across the border in Mexico. He was selling people's daughters and sisters to brothels in Chihuahua. Some of them were children. The filthiest business you ever heard of. They were killed, some of them. He was lucky not to hang.'

The two men looked at Flynn impassively. One of them smiled. It was obvious that neither cared about any of this, their sensibilities having been blunted by living and working in an environment such as existed in this town. Docherty said, 'I didn't hang though, did I? Didn't serve any twenty years either, comes to that.'

'No, you broke out with a few others and killed a guard while you were doing so. You'll hang for that when once you're back in custody.'

'That what you're doing here, Marshal Flynn?' asked Docherty with unfeigned curiosity. 'Hoping to bring me back to face justice?'

'No. Like I said, I'm not a marshal anymore. My business here is of what you might term a purely personal nature. I often wondered what had become of you, Docherty. I might've guessed you'd still be mixed up in dirt and beastliness.'

Flynn noted with some satisfaction that this had struck home and that Docherty's affected air of non-chalance was wearing thin. The boyish smile was looking more like a rictus grin than anything indicative of humour, and he said to Flynn, 'All right, we've had our fun, now let's talk straight.'

He couldn't help saying wryly in reply to this appeal, 'You talking straight, Docherty? Well, that will be a novelty at any rate!'

'You've a choice. You know I can't set you free. If nothing else, I know what a sanctimonious and unforgiving bastard you are. Even if you're no longer a lawman, you'd still go straight off and lay an information against me, get folk stirred up into issuing a warrant and coming to look for me here.'

'Then what?'

'If you tell me honestly what brings you here and give me chapter and verse about any friends you come here with, I'll promise that you'll die easy. Just a single shot and it'll all be over.'

'If I don't?'

'Then I'll make you another promise. I'll make your death so frightful that anybody who hears of it will walk in fear and trembling of my name, and it'll be a byword for what happens to those as try and fool with me.'

*

92

Three stores in Larkspur sold powder and shot. Moses Jackson was well aware that it would cause eyebrows to rise were he to attempt to buy all the powder he required in one place. Brady had more than enough money on him and probably calculated quite correctly that any expenditure at this stage would be more than compensated for in the coming weeks, as his newspaper ran a series of thrilling articles, headed perhaps, 'RESCUING GIRLS FROM THE VICE DENS OF KENTUCKY' or, 'A NEWSPAPERMAN'S CRUSADE'.

In addition to his subsistence farming, Jackson had a sideline that took him from home from time to time. This was as an expert in laying charges and clearing rocks away. He was sometimes engaged for this purpose by railroads, faced with a rocky outcrop that obstructed the route of their latest line. He was known as a man who knew the best way to tackle problems of that sort without risking life and limb. Quarries employed him from time to time, too, and he had a good reputation there. Taking down a few buildings would be a challenge, but one which he felt sure that he would be able to rise to. After acquiring four pounds in one place and three each in two other stores, Jackson thought that he was ready to essay something quite new in the blasting line. He might have wished that he had somebody working with him upon whom he could rely for help, but there it was. You didn't always get what you wanted in this world, and the young fellow who had supplied him with the wherewithal to purchase the black powder was, from all that Jackson was able to see, as soft as butter and would be no more use than a woman in an enterprise like this.

Buying the powder was a straightforward matter, although there was no denying that purchasing a keg containing four pounds of the stuff caused the clerk's eyebrows to raise. It seemed at first that acquiring fuse would be impossible. All three stores where Jackson bought black powder denied having any such commodity on the premises. It was only after Moses Jackson told a long, convoluted and untruthful tale about being engaged at a quarry and needing the fuse urgently that one of the storekeepers instituted a search in his backroom, which unearthed two feet of stuff. 'You sure that's all you got?' asked Jackson dubiously. 'No more anywhere?'

'Listen, friend,' said the man behind the counter, 'I already spent ten minutes of my time rooting around for this here. Take it or leave it.'

'Oh, I'll take it,' said Jackson hastily. He turned to Jake Brady and said, 'Would you settle up with the gentleman?'

As they left the store, Brady asked, 'What if Flynn isn't in that house any more? What then?'

'I reckon as we should cross that bridge when we come to it.'

For all that the newspaperman was better educated and more in tune with political matters and economics than the dirt farmer walking along at his side, Jackson had a more extensive knowledge of the less salubrious side of life. He had figured out that the life of a marshal, or ex-marshal, who had been poking around and asking awkward questions wasn't worth a dime in a place such as this, and although he didn't care all that much for Jed Flynn as a human person, he needed him to carry out his own aims. He said, 'I already seen a couple of spots which'll do fine for what I got in mind. You want to go back into one o' them stores and get us a quart of lamp oil? I didn't want to buy it at the same time as the powder; it might've roused suspicions.'

'What the deuce do you want with lamp oil?'

'You'll see.'

Had it not been for the fact that he was already up to his neck in this mire, then it is by no means impossible that Jack Brady might have tried to back out of any further part in the whole business. He was, however, uneasily aware that if those men who had marched off Marshal Flynn at gunpoint found out that he was in cahoots with Brady, that he himself might be the next target for their attentions, a circumstance that he was eager to avoid. He accordingly bought the lamp oil. Jackson had begged a hemp sack from one of the stores, in which he had stowed the three kegs of powder. Jack Brady therefore carried the flagon of oil himself. He wondered if those passing them in the street were suspicious at all of them.

*

Before taking active steps to secure Flynn's coopera-
tion, Michael Docherty was in the mood for a little
boasting, which is seldom a good idea when you're
talking to a man who has spent the whole of his adult
life in upholding the law. He said, 'Me and two
others run this town by our own selves, with no interference from anybody in the world, do you realize
that? Nobody from the state, no federal authorities,
nobody at all. I make tell that we've a vigilance committee, which in a sense we have, and since we save
everybody the cost of law keeping and so on, we get
pretty much left alone. Have to grease a few palms
away over in the state capital, of course, but that's just
like paying taxes. The understanding is that there's
no crime around here, nobody troubled, no violent
disorder, you get the picture?'

Jedediah Flynn got the picture only too well, and
he writhed with impotent fury at the level of corrup-
tion required to condone such a pesthole as this and
turn a blind eye to some of the greatest wickedness
imaginable. He made a personal vow that if ever he
were to be free of the toils here, then he would come
back as soon as he was able and clean the place up.

'I'm sorry not to oblige, Docherty, but my business
here is my own. It really doesn't need to concern you.
But I give you my word that I had no idea when I
stepped off the train that you were here.'

'And will you give your word that you won't tell a
living soul in the future that you know now where
I'm to be found?'

'No, I can't make any promises on that score.'

'It's as I thought. Did you come here alone?'

'I can't help you there, I'm afraid.'

'We'll try that, shall we?' Turning to the men who were guarding Flynn, Michael Docherty said, 'You, Dave. Go fetch me a length of rope. Stout, mind.' When the man had left the room, Docherty said, 'You chose the hard way, Marshal. Just recollect that when you're screaming for mercy.'

'I doubt you'll live long enough to hear such a thing,' replied Flynn equably. 'We'll see who's screaming for mercy when I come to watch you hang.'

After Flynn's hands were securely and painfully lashed together, with such vigour that the circulation of blood to his hands was impeded, he was taken from the house at gunpoint and marched to a squat, stone-built structure at the far end of the garden away from the house. The interior of this little hut was dank and gloomy. Along the walls were wheelbarrows, spades and other tools, which suggested that one purpose of this single-storey building was as a storage space for gardening requisites. Flynn noted that a large, iron hook had been driven into one of the roof-beams, perhaps ten feet from the ground. He soon discovered the reason for this item, as the two men following Docherty's orders lifted him up and somehow contrived to slip his bound hands over the hook. When they had competed this manoeuvre, Jed Flynn found that he was hanging from the ceiling, with his toes an inch or two from the dirt floor of the shed. The pain in his wrists was already excruciating, and this was before any additional means were being exerted in order to compel him to talk.

'I hope you're comfortable,' said Docherty ironically. 'It's time to see if you're as tough as everybody used to make out when they talked about you. Folk in the penitentiary always said that you were as hard as all-get-out-and-push, but me, I thought all along that if ever I could have you at my mercy, you'd turn out to be a craven dog who'd beg for his life. What do you say?'

'What do I say? I say that you're a damned coward who'd be afraid to face me in a fair fight, man to man. It's one thing when you're abusing and mistreating little girls, but you durst not stand up to a real man. All you white slavers got yellow bellies.'

The words were no sooner our of Flynn's mouth than Michael Docherty had snatched up a pick handle which was leaning against the wall and this he rammed sharply into the helpless man's stomach. The natural impulse of somebody treated so is of course to double up in agony and gasp for breath, but hanging by his wrists as he was, this was quite impossible for Flynn. He writhed helplessly and struggled to suck air into his lungs.

Docherty had evidently had some experience of inflicting pain in this way, for he did not simply rain blows with the length of hickory wood, one after the other, but instead waited for each individual assault to linger on and reach its fullest effect, before striking again. This was far more effective than a flurry of uncontrolled violence. After waiting until Flynn had regained his breath, Docherty asked in an amicable way, 'What brought you to Larkspur?' When he received no answer, he enquired in the same tone, 'Did you come here alone or with companions?' Receiving no reply to these questions, Docherty cracked the other man on the shin and then waited for a few seconds before repeating the questions. This process went on for what seemed to Flynn an interminable length of time. Each time he refused to answer, he received another savage blow on a sensitive part of his anatomy.

At one point during his interrogation, the pain reached such a pitch that Jed Flynn, for the first time in his life, was on the point of passing out. He began mumbling indistinctly and the three men standing around were in hopes that he was now willing to answer the questions, although unable to formulate the words clearly enough for them to understand. A bucket of water was thrown over him, which it was thought might revive him sufficiently to make his speech a little more comprehensible. As a matter of fact, their victim had been murmuring a plea to the Almighty for deliverance, rather than attempting to betray those with whom he arrived in the town. When he was a little more clear-headed, he raised his voice and began again to recite the twenty-third

Psalm, 'The Lord is my shepherd, I shall not want. . . .'

It might have gone ill with Jedediah Flynn, for this display of piety was not at all to the taste of the man who was questioning him, and had there not been a sudden and unexpected interruption, there is no telling how things might have turned out. Docherty's patience was all worn away and it is possible that he would have fallen upon the prisoner at this point and beaten him to death, but from outside came a most extraordinary sound, like a tremendous clap of thunder near at hand. This was followed swiftly by another roar, which was by the sound of it, a little further away. The day was bright and sunny, without so much as a wisp of cloud in the sky. Whatever else that almighty crash had been, it surely was not thunder.

CHAPTER 6

Jack Brady was growing increasingly unsure of the wisdom of his remaining in Moses Jackson's company. The farmer was, from all that he was able to collect, about to embark upon some course of action that might result in death and destruction on a not inconsiderable scale. As they walked towards the edge of town, he said, 'I'm not sure about this, Mister Jackson. Can you promise me that nobody will be hurt by what you are proposing to do?'

'Can't promise anything like that,' said Moses Jackson. 'Most of my blasting has been in what you might call out of the way places. Couldn't say what will happen in a town.'

'But you'll at least do your best to minimise harm?'

'Oh yes,' said Jackson, 'I'll surely do that.'

Once they were within sight of the large house to which Flynn had been taken at gunpoint, Jackson said, 'I aim for to set off three mines. One in that barn or whatever you might call it, just here, and the

101

other in the stable block across the street from that house. I'm going to spring the other at the gateway, so's to allow us entrance. Let's get in this barn, out of sight.'

Brady noticed that although the man he was helping had hitherto been the most taciturn and uncommunicative of individuals, now that he was engaged on a job of work in his own line, he appeared to come to life. The editor of the *Clayton County Advertiser* had the horrible suspicion that the fellow actually enjoyed blowing things up and that he had an almost academic interest in seeing the effects of the gunpowder, which he usually used on boulders and rocks, and seeing what it might do to buildings.

Once inside the old barn, which must be a leftover relic from the time a few years ago when Larkspur consisted of no more than a half-dozen soddies and a blacksmith's forge, Jackson took the flask of lamp oil from the other man and began splashing it liberally around the wooden walls, remarking as he did so, 'We want a good blaze here, something to draw a crowd.'

'What use is that to us?'

'Whoever lives in yon house is what you might term a man of importance, I'd say. Happen he and the others'll come here to see what's doing.'

'You hope to lure them out?'

'That's it.'

Jack Brady felt an unwilling admiration for the illiterate farmer. He might not be able to read and write, but he had certainly grasped quicker than Brady what would be the best way of achieving their ends here. It was a hazardous scheme for all concerned, but it might just work. He said, 'So if you can blow the gate off its hinges, and the master of the house runs out to investigate, then we can go in and look for Marshal Flynn. What if anybody is left behind to guard him?'

Jackson gestured at the ancient scattergun that he had left leaning against the wall and said stolidly, 'Then I'll kill such a one.'

Few people, other than architects and builders, ever stop to consider what stresses and strains a house is constructed to withstand. The chief force likely to act on the structure of any building, apart from gravity that is, is of course wind blowing against it. This can be enough to knock down a flimsily built house, even one made of bricks and mortar. Walls are braced to withstand pushing from without, but hardly any attempt is made to resist forces operating from within a building. After all, when did anybody hear of winds blowing up in somebody's bedroom or kitchen? It is for this reason that a relatively small charge of explosives can wreak an inordinate amount of damage to the average building if placed internally; it is simply not made to withstand any pressure at all coming from inside. All of this meant that the ten pounds of powder of which Jackson possessed would very likely accomplish his purpose.

'We needs must move very fast once I set light to

the fuse,' said Jackson, in the same slow way that he might have remarked upon inclement weather, 'Else the two of us'll be blown to kingdom come.'

'How great a delay will there be?' asked Brady, a little nervously. 'We don't want to kill ourselves.'

'Ten seconds or thereabouts.'

'God almighty, that barely gives us time to get clear!'

'It's plenty. Don't fret so.'

After emptying the content of the flagon of lamp oil over the wooden walls of the old barn, Jackson fixed a third of the fuse that he had purchased into one of the three-pound, wooden kegs of black powder. This he set upright, next to one of the walls that he had covered with the flammable liquid. Then, checking that nobody was about, he led Jack Brady to the stable opposite the house in which they were interested. After forcing an entry at the back, he set another of his mines on the floor, saying, 'Two down, one to go.'

Because the mansion was on the very edge of town, away from all the saloons, gambling spots and hurdy houses, there was nobody around to observe all the activity. Before leaving the stable, Moses Jackson rubbed his chin thoughtfully and said, 'If we get the marshal free, we'll have to hole up near here for a spell. Just for a couple o' hours, you know.'

'Where do you suggest, Mister Jackson?'

'I see a privy over yonder. We could all three of us squeeze in there and I doubt anyone'd suspect us being there.'

Brady said nothing, but thought privately that just when he thought things could not possible get any more unpleasant, there was always one more surprise in store. The prospect of spending hours in a derelict privy with Jackson and Marshal Flynn was very far from being an attractive one. From the sardonic look on the farmer's face, it seemed likely that he had guessed what the journalist was thinking, for he said, 'Never mind. Happen we'll both be killed when I spring this mine, then we won't need to worry about such matters.'

Jackson's plan was a simple one that, if it came off, might prove to be devastatingly effective. He would first start a fire in the old barn. Once the lamp oil had caught flame, it would light the fuse on the keg of powder. Before that happened, though, it was planned that the fuses on the other two mines would be lit and that the three explosions would follow each other in quick succession. As all this was explained to Brady he began to tremble in fear, and Moses Jackson took pity upon him. He said, 'You run off now and hide in that privy, and I'll be there with our partner, if all works out to plan.'

Blushing red with shame, Jack Brady shuffled off to hide. There were, he thought as he opened the door of the privy and closed it behind him, worse things in the world than being embarrassed at somebody finding out what a coward you are.

Once he had got rid of the young man whom he

saw as more of a hindrance than a help, Jackson set to. He walked casually from the stable to the old barn and piled some scraps of paper, twigs and small pieces of fire against the wall where he had splashed the oil. Then he struck a Lucifer and kindled a little blaze. Having done so, he then made tracks back to the stable, lit the fuse on the keg there and sprinted across the street to do the same with the little barrel of powder that he had wedged between the iron gate and its stone gatepost. Luckily, there was still nobody around. Knowing that there was only a matter of seconds before the area where he stood would be under a rain of bricks and stones, Moses Jackson bestirred himself and ran as fast as he was able, down the street and away from the place where the explosions would shortly take place.

There were no other houses hereabouts, so far from the centre of town, just a few walls and broken-down and deserted soddys. After pounding along for four or five seconds, Jackson threw himself down behind a tumbled down wall. He was only just in time, for there came almost immediately afterwards the most tremendous blast, followed almost at once by a second. He had always taken good care, both in the army and later, when hiring himself out as a demolition expert, not to be too close to the seat of an explosion, but this was a sight nearer than was comfortable. As he lay there, face down with his hands clasped over the back of his head to provide some protection for that vital part of his body, a rain of stones, pieces of wood, chunks of ironwork and fragments of brick landed around him. Then there came the concussion, which he felt through the shaking of the ground, of a third explosion – that in the barn.

The whole area was covered with a white cloud of powdered plaster and mortar. For this, Jackson was heartily thankful, for almost before the echoes of the three blasts had died away, he heard angry shouting from the grounds of the grand house. Just as he had hoped, but until now had not known for sure, the men who came running through the shattered gateway turned left and made for the blazing remains of the wooden barn. He counted three of them. The cloud of dust gave him a little cover, so as soon as the men had headed off to see what had started the fire, Jackson unslung his scattergun and, holding it at high port, went loping into the grounds of the house. It would not be true to say that the poverty-stricken and hardworking farmer had wholly forgotten the ultimate object of the exercise – that is to say the rescue of his daughter and her restitution to the bosom of her family – but he had surely become bound up in this little adventure to no small degree. There could be no doubt that as he charged across the well-manicured garden in search of a target that he felt more alive than he had since the end of the war. If he'd thought deeply on the matter, he would have agreed that for the first time in years, he was actually enjoying life.

As Jackson neared the house, he heard a man's voice shout, 'I'm here!' The call for help seemed to come from a brick-built shed at back of the garden. He ran as fast as he could in that direction, cocking one barrel of the shotgun as he neared the place. The door was ajar and, kicking it open, he charged in, almost bumping into one of the vigilantes he had earlier seen strike Marshal Flynn with his musket butt.

The man who had been left to guard the helpless prisoner was hugely surprised to see somebody lurch through the door of the shed. He began to raise his rifle, but Moses Jackson had the advantage of him; he was already expecting to have to kill somebody. The roar of the twelve-gauge in the confined space was deafening and it was at once plain that there would be no need for the second barrel. The shot, which had consisted of bits of old nails and other small pieces of metal in addition to buckshot, had torn a gaping hole in the other man's belly. As he fell to the floor, Jackson noted with interest that portions of his intestines were protruding from the wound. From near at hand, he heard a man's voice ask irritably, 'You going to stand there admiring your handiwork or are you planning to get me down from here?'

After hoisting Flynn down from the hook, it was the work of seconds to slash him free of his bonds with the jack-knife that Jackson invariably carried about his person. The sudden restoration of circulation to his extremities caused the former marshal a

108

good deal of pain. He rubbed his hands vigorously and said, 'We best not linger. I guess those bangs were your work?'

'They were.'

'I thought something was going on. I'll thank you at greater length another time, but for now we had best shift ourselves.' He bent down and took the dead man's pistol and rifle.

'Can you walk unaided?' asked Jackson uncertainly, and received a look of impatience for a reply. The two men hurried from the shed and made their way to where the remains of the fancy iron gate lay twisted upon the ground. There was no sign of anybody else, of which both men were heartily glad. Jackson said, 'Our friend's hiding over the way in a privy. I figure we're better staying put near the scene. Those villains'll expect us to flee. They won't search overmuch near at hand.'

Jed Flynn shot the other an appraising look, one mingled with admiration. He said, 'I'm more grateful than I can tell. I reckon you weren't always a farmer?'

'I reckon not,' said Jackson laconically.

It surely was a tight squeeze for the three of them to fit into the old, wooden privy hut, but they succeeded. Outside, they could hear men shouting in the distance and also the sound of running feet, sometimes far away and at other times near at hand. It was just as Jackson had thought. It did not occur to anybody that the men who had set the mines and freed their prisoner would simply have stayed put in the vicinity. It had been early evening when Flynn had been captured and now it was full dark before the three of them took the chance of emerging from their unsavoury refuge.

'Those boys will have spread word about me by now,' said Flynn, 'by which I mean my appearance and such. I need a change of clothes at the least. Not to mention where we can't roam the town like this as an armed band; we stand out by a mile.' There was some truth in what he said, for he had a pistol tucked in his belt and a carbine under his arm. For his part, Moses Jackson was carrying his scattergun at the ready, and he too was sporting a most large and noticeable pistol. The odd one out of the group was Jack Brady, who was not only unarmed, but looked quite respectable when compared to his two companions.

Brady became aware of the others looking at him expectantly and said, 'What would you have me do? I confess freely, I'm not a man of action and I'm not ashamed to own it.'

Flynn felt a little sorrow for the younger man, who had come here looking for a good story for his newspaper and was now embroiled in a minor war. He said kindly, 'All you need to do, Mister Brady, is rent us a room at a cheap place and then let us in through a back door or something, so that nobody sees us plain. If you could change clothes with me, that too would be a great help.'

'Suppose they mistake me for you?'

'I don't look for that to happen. We don't look alike, but they might have described to others what I was wearing. This black outfit's a mite noticeable on me.'

Jack Brady was torn between a mortal fear of being beaten or shot and the realization that he was slap-bang in the middle of the biggest story of his life. This was a tale that could be serialised in the big papers on the east coast. Then he would be able to dine out for the rest of his days on the anecdotes that this adventure was generating. He said, 'I'll do it. Give me fifteen minutes to get to the centre of town and the same before I'm back again.'

While they waited in the darkness of an empty lot between Docherty's house and Main Street, Flynn said to the farmer, 'You saved my life back there, but then you already know that.'

'Did you tell them anything?'

Flynn chuckled and said, 'No, but that's not through bravery. If I'd have opened up about every-thing, they'd have killed me as soon as I had finished. Throwing you to the wolves wouldn't have saved my life.'

Moses Jackson grunted and said, 'You make light of it, but I don't think you'd have betrayed us in any case. You're not that kind.'

'Maybe.'

It was a little over half an hour before Brady returned with the news that he had rented a room for the night in a very run down and disreputable lodging house. There was a back door that he would open for them to let them enter the house without scrutiny.

By skulking through alleyways and behind buildings, the three men gained the rear of the lodging house without incident. Jack Brady went round to the front, entered in a respectable fashion and then swiftly went to the back of the house to let in the others, who slipped unnoticed up the stairs to the room that Brady had acquired for the night. There, he and Flynn changed clothes. Mercifully, there was little difference in stature between the two of them, although Flynn found the other man's pants a little tight in the waist. Then the newspaperman went downstairs to order some food and coffee to take up to his room. The woman running the place concluded that either her new guest was harbouring a tapeworm in his belly or he was the most greedy and immoderate eater whom she had ever entertained under her roof. He took enough food up to his room for three men!

Once their stomachs were full and Flynn's appearance had been modified a tad by switching clothes with the journalist, the three of them began to plan what next to do. Or, to be strictly accurate, Jackson and Flynn reasoned the case out, while Jack Brady listened carefully and took unobtrusive notes. He could contribute nothing useful to the discussion, but at least he could chronicle faithfully what had been said.

'Here's how I see things,' said Flynn. 'Michael Docherty, who I sent to gaol for twenty years and is now wanted for murder, has as nice a little setup here as you could hope to find. This town has so far slipped between the cracks of law enforcement, as you might say. They tell the regular law that they have a vigilance committee keeping order and because this is not a haunt for the lawless, and there's no killing or robbing in the vicinity, the law elsewhere are content to let matters be.' He looked up and said, 'Everybody see it the same way?'

Neither Jackson nor Brady offered any remark and so he continued. 'Point is, Docherty knows now that I am around. Apart from the fact that he owes me an ill turn, he'll be sweating blood, hoping that I don't go bearing tales to anybody of what I know about him. He'd be on the run again and this time I don't think he'd get so far. His life's at stake, so he'll take any risks to kill me. He knows too that I ain't alone and that'll be a worry to him as well.'

'Which is all very interesting,' said Moses Jackson, 'but doesn't get me any the closer to getting my little girl home.'

'If Docherty thinks, and I believe he does, that I am here snooping around in an official capacity, then by now I'd be making my way back to a big city and swearing out a warrant for his arrest. He's no reason to know that this is by way of being a private venture and that I didn't come here looking for him. It's a coincidence, but he won't see it that way.'

113

'I'm a patient man, Marshal Flynn, but you're being wordy. How will we get my Abigail home?'

'Way I see it, Docherty's like to leave town for a while, just to be sure to avoid any posses I might've raised that comes looking for him. But he's a man to combine such a trip with business, 'less'n he's changed greatly since I last knew him. I'd stake a heap on him taking a few girls south with him, to make his absence pay for itself.'

'How's that?' asked Jack Brady. 'I don't rightly understand you.'

'I took him for running a racket where he was recruiting silly, vain girls for an outfit as went by the name of the Spanish-American Entertainment Company. There was no coercion, any more than there is with the hurdy houses; the girls were keen as mustard to go where he directed them. He promised them careers as singers, actresses and I don't know what all else. He paid their fare down to El Paso and then took 'em across the Rio Grande into Mexico. Once there, they wound up in cathouses. There was, still is like as not, a hefty premium on white girls as has not before lain with a man. Virgins, you know.'

'You think he'll try the same stunt now?' asked Moses Jackson, his face pale and strained. 'Why, he might take my own child with him!'

'We're hoping he does,' said Flynn, a hard and deadly look in his eyes. 'Freeing those girls and getting them away from this town'd be a mighty hard

114

row to hoe. Other hand, if they were on board a rail-road train, with a heap of other passengers and only Docherty and a few others ... why, the job would undertake itself.'

'It would?' asked Brady. 'Maybe it's me, but I don't see that at all.'

Jackson cut in at this point, a curious smile playing around the corners of his mouth. He said, 'What the marshal has in mind, I reckon, is that him and me could work together and kill this here Docherty and his boys, and he wouldn't have a band of armed men to aid him in the fight like he would if we tried the same trick here in Larkspur.'

'I see we understand each other well enough,' said Flynn, 'except where I hope to avoid bloodshed if possible.'

'We all hope that, as God knows,' said Jackson piously, 'but I don't look for those boys to deliver up the girls we want, other than under a threat.'

The newspaper editor, who was catching up with what the others seemed to be planning, said, 'But aren't the odds against both the girls you fellows have an interest in being taken off to El Paso, even if that is what's planned? Are they particular beauties?'

'I couldn't say,' replied Jed Flynn. 'Not having had the pleasure of meeting either of them. I'll warrant though that they're virgins, not having yet had time to being in this town and get up to any debased activities. No, if I'm right, then those girls will be among those he takes with him.'

Shortly after this conversation, Moses Jackson went off to visit the hurdy house that they had not yet been in. He saw neither his daughter nor Mary Shanahan there. Just to be sure, he went back to the other two hurdy houses they had been in before and established that the girls whom they were seeking were not to be found there either. If they had in fact arrived in Larkspur, then they had not been set to work immediately in a hurdy house. This tended to confirm in Jackson's mind the idea advanced by Marshal Flynn, that their value to the man who had arranged for them to journey here might lie perhaps in their unsullied state.

After murdering a guard and escaping from the penitentiary in Louisiana, the first practical step take by Michael Docherty to avoid the unfortunate consequences of his actions had been to change his name and begin calling himself Flaherty, rather than Docherty. He had secreted away a large part of the profits of his Spanish-American Entertainment Corporation and used these to buy his way into a hurdy house in Kentucky, far away from the scene of his previous activities. This investment prospered and after two years, Docherty was ready for the move to Larkspur, up until then a sleepy hamlet consisting of a dozen ramshackle old buildings, a few old barns and a blacksmith's forge. He sank his money into financing the building of a modest establishment, where men could drink, gamble, watch scantily clad dancers and, if they wished to do so, take these young women upstairs after the show. It had been a gamble, but one which had paid off magnificently. Men passing through were at first his bread and butter, but then came those who visited Larkspur for no other reason than the pleasures of the flesh that it offered. Docherty had not started alone in this enterprise, for his capital was not sufficient for all that he envisioned, and so he had teamed up with two other men who had the same general idea. None of the three of them by themselves had enough money to build and furnish that first house and so they had, from the start, been bound to each other not by mutual liking and affection, but rather by bonds of financial interest. It was these three men who now ran Larkspur. Because he had put in more of the starting capital than the other two, Docherty, or Flaherty as everybody now knew him, had in time come to be known by those in the town as 'the boss', a fact that irritated the other two men who had invested heavily in the town and caused considerable ill-feeling between them and the 'boss'.

When three ruthless and unscrupulous men band together in this way for a common purpose, there will always be the constant and nagging fear in the mind of each of them that the other two are planning to cheat them or dispose of them, thus increasing the profits for the remaining pair. Docherty felt this anxiety keenly and the arrival of a lawman in town that knew his real name and possessed enough information to see him hanged was like a lightning bolt from a clear blue sky. He would not put it past his fellow bosses to capitalise on this unlooked-for development and conspire to see him arrested and executed. For this reason, it was imperative from Docherty's point of view that neither of the other men learned what had happened. It was a blow to discover that Flynn was evidently not working alone and had been freed by some person or persons unknown, but a great relief in another sense because it had ended with the death of Dave Freeman. Only two people, other than Docherty himself, had known that day that he was in reality none other than Michael Docherty, a man on the run from a twenty-year sentence and also wanted for murder. One was dead, and if Docherty had anything to say on the matter then the other would soon be following to the grave. It had not escaped his noticed that when Flynn had spoken his correct name, there had been a glint of interest in Jim Mortimer's face and it was probably a question of time until the man made some use of this information. Either he would try and blackmail Docherty or he would bear the tale to one of the other bosses. It was therefore urgent to engineer Mortimer's death as soon as could be conveniently arranged.

The morning after Jed Flynn had been captured and then escaped, Docherty called round to the rooming house where Jim Mortimer was living. He was all affability as he congratulated the younger man warmly on having caught Flynn and brought him to the house. He said, 'I reckon as you deserve a little break after that. A sign of my appreciation, if you like.'

Mortimer, who had been planning the best way to put the bite on his boss by using the information acquired during Flynn's interrogation, was pleasantly surprised to find himself being spoken to so fairly. He said, 'Why, that's right nice of you, Mister Flaherty. What was it you had in mind?'

'How does a trip south to El Paso sound? Maybe even crossing the border and spending a few days letting the badger loose in Mexico.'

The prospect was an alluring one, and Mortimer smiled at the idea of touring a few of the cathouses to be found across the Rio Grande. Some of those places catered for the most exotic tastes, providing delights that would not have been tolerated in even the most liberal and easy-going towns in the United States. He said, 'Sounds good to me. When do we start?'

'This very day. Can you be at the depot in an hour and a half?'

'You bet your life.'

It did not escape Michael Docherty's notice that his underling was now addressing him in a most familiar fashion, as though they were equals and not master and servant. In another day or so, he supposed that Mortimer would be calling him 'Mister Docherty' and then hastily correcting himself, as a means to remind them both what he knew. This would be most worrisome and alarming if Jim Mortimer was likely to live longer than twenty-four hours, which Docherty strongly doubted.

To Moses Jackson and Jack Brady, Flynn's ability to predict the future actions of a man with such uncanny precision appeared almost supernatural. He had told them that the man he knew as Docherty would be leaving Larkspur that day and, lo and behold, here they were now at the railroad depot, watching as Docherty and another man shepherded five young girls aboard the westbound service, which was due to depart in just a quarter of an hour. One of the girls was Jackson's daughter, and it was all that Flynn could do to restrain her father and prevent him from rushing over, killing the two men and rescuing his daughter on the spot. Gripping the irate man's arm, Flynn said in an urgent undertone, 'Don't be a damned fool. You'd be caught and strung up in next to no time. Those villains rule this place, at least for now. We'll board the self-same train and then deal with the matter when we're clear of this cesspit.'

'Him you call Docherty,' replied Jackson, turning a cold eye on the former marshal, 'He's mine. I'm a goin' to kill him myself.'

'We need to catch our hare,' said Flynn, with a

grim smile, 'before we start planning how to cook it. And I told you, no killing at all, unless we have no choice.'

Jed Flynn and the others were standing by the side of a wooden shack used for storing spades and other tools used about the tracks. They had, from this vantage point, a perfect and unobstructed view of the whole depot. Once it was certain that the girls they sought were getting on the train, Brady was despatched to purchase tickets for them all. He was beginning to grow a little irked at the fact that he was now single-handedly financing the whole entire enterprise, but Flynn assured him that if they achieved their purpose, then there would be reward money to come for catching Michael Docherty whether or not he died in the process. 'Tidy sum, too,' said Flynn. 'Better than a thousand dollars from what I recollect.'

'And I can have it all?' asked the journalist suspiciously.

'I've no interest in it. All that Jackson here wants is his daughter safe and sound. So, yes, it's all yours, if we succeed in what we are about to attempt.'

Thus placated, the young man went off to buy the tickets. When he was out of earshot, Moses Jackson said, 'That true? About the reward money, I mean.'

'It's true enough. You think I'd lie about it?'

'I think you'd do or say anything to see that Docherty caught.'

There was little answer to be made to this assertion, it being as accurate a summing-up of the state of affairs as could be, and so Flynn said nothing.

CHAPTER 7

The girls on the train were as happy and excited as if they had been children going to a Sunday school picnic. They chattered and giggled as though the whole thing was a glorious lark. Watching them with an eye honed in such matters, Docherty was judging which of them could be dressed up to look younger than their actual age. One of them could probably be tricked out as a twelve-year-old when they were across the border. There was a place he knew of that specialised in providing services for men who preferred the exceedingly young and tender. Men with a taste for such things crossed over from the States and were prepared to part with fabulous sums of money to satisfy their depraved appetites. Abigail Jackson caught him staring at her speculatively and asked pertly, 'What are you looking at me like that for? Have I a smut on my nose or something?'

'Nothing of the sort, my dear,' replied Docherty gallantly. 'I was just thinking how fresh and young you look. Why, you're a delight to rest the eye upon.'

The foolish girl giggled and simpered before falling back into whispering to her new friends. She was surely finding life over the last few days a sight more entertaining than the drudgery of the farm to which she was accustomed. It is by no means impossible that even if she had been apprised of the reality of her situation, she might even then have preferred to stay with Docherty and the others rather than go back to her dull and wearisome home.

Jedediah Flynn and his two companions boarded the rear coach of the train, it having been observed that the girls whom they were intent upon freeing had been taken aboard further to the front. Flynn had the pistol that he had acquired from the dead man tucked into his belt at the back and covered by the jacket that he had borrowed from Brady. He hoped in this way to present a law-abiding and innocuous appearance until the time came to strike. The newspaper editor was still wearing Flynn's clothes, which made him look a little more raffish and dishevelled than was usual with him. He had no weapon at all and his role was simply to be that of an observer. As for Jackson, the farmer looked rough and dangerous, with not only the Walker at his hip, but also the scattergun in his hand. One or two passengers, when once they had glanced at him, chose to move further down the carriage so as to be as far from the unprepossessing figure as possible. Once the train started from the depot, with a clanking of couplings, a mournful whistle and clouds of white steam, Moses Jackson and Flynn bent their heads close together and discussed the best way of going about their task.

'I want no shooting, unless we are ourselves fired upon,' said Flynn. 'You understand me?

'Just as you say, Marshal,' replied the other meekly. 'I'll follow your lead, you know.'

Flynn started hard at Jackson, hoping to impress upon him by a fierce scowl that he meant what he said. The other man contrived to look as harmless and inoffensive as a newly born babe, but the marshal was not deceived. Still, there was little to be done, for he certainly needed somebody to back him in this enterprise and Jackson was the only one who fitted the bill. He would not have wanted to rely upon the newspaperman in a tense situation. Jackson said, 'How do you say we should go about things?'

'First off is where we leave that shotgun o' your'n here with our friend. The sight of you bearing down towards them carrying that will set all manner of alarms ringing. I aim for the two of us to stroll up as casual as you like and then to draw down on them when we're right on top of 'em.'

'You think they'll recognize you?'

'We'll have to hope not.'

'Mind,' said Jackson thoughtfully, 'they certainly won't know me. What say I go on ahead and then wait behind them before you approach? That way, they'll be caught between two fires.'

Flynn thought this proposal over for a spell and said at last, 'There's somewhat in it, but then again there's the chance of us shooting each other if it comes to gunfire and we're both at opposite ends of the coach. No, let's do it my way.'

'Just as you say.'

Over the course of the last few days, ever since he had become caught up in this business in fact, Jed Flynn had all but forgotten about the notion of taking holy orders. At the back of his mind, of course, he knew that his plan was to continue on to Lafayette after restoring Mary Shanahan to her mother, but all thoughts of religious duty had faded away in the danger of the pursuit that he had undertaken. He really hoped that he would be able to deal with Docherty and his partner without the shedding of blood, and then it would simply be a matter of returning to Harker's Crossing, getting young Mary home and then heading north again. Already, though, the thought of that lawless town that he had lately left was preying upon his mind. Surely something would have to be done about that? It wasn't right for a town to exist in that way, with only the wicked running the place. Deep inside, Jedediah Flynn knew that he would not be able to rest easy until he had cleaned up that place a little.

Flynn started, as he realized that Moses Jackson had said something. He said, 'Beg pardon, I'm sure. I was miles away. What did you say?'

'I said that I see no cause to sit here waiting. If

we're going to do this thing, then we might as well get on and do it.'

'You speak truly,' said Flynn and got to his feet.

A famous poet once expressed the view that 'the best-laid plans of mice and men go oft astray', and the veracity of this assertion was amply demonstrated that day as Jed Flynn and Moses Jackson walked along the aisle of that railroad coach to take down the men who were, at that very moment, trying to sell a bunch of young girls into virtual slavery. At first, everything went as smoothly as could be. The two of them walked along the coach in which they were travelling, opened the door and then hopped across the coupling and entered the next coach. In this way, they moved down the train to the coach that contained the men in whom they were interested.

Jackson and Flynn opened the door at the end of the coach through which they had just walked and then, having closed it behind them, stepped over the coupling between the two coaches and opened the door leading to the next carriage. It was then that things took a turn for the worse, because the conductor, a fussy old fellow with a bristling white moustache was right by the door when they stepped through it and into the coach. He said in a loud and irritable voice, 'Now then, now then, what's all this here? You men are a little old to be playing such games, running from coach to coach. Ain't you ashamed of yourselves?'

Feeling that it might shut up the old man and

make things easier, Flynn said quietly, 'Hush up now. I'm a marshal and I'm in pursuit of a suspect.' He made as though to brush past the conductor, who was not about to have his own authority reduced to nothing in this way.

'Marshal, is it?' asked the conductor loudly. 'Let's be seeing your badge.'

Halfway down the coach, the word 'marshal' caught the immediate attention of Michael Docherty, who was sitting with his back to the scene unfolding behind him. He craned his head around and at once recognized Jed Flynn as the man disputing with the guard. Upon which, he nudged Jim Mortimer, who was sitting next to him in the window seat and said, 'We got trouble!'

Turning around and raising himself slightly, so that he could peer over the back of his seat, Mortimer said, 'Shit! What now?'

Already, Docherty was reaching inside his jacket for the pistol that he kept beneath his armpit in a chamois leather holster. As soon as she caught sight of the weapon being drawn, Abigail Jackson gave a loud scream of terror; she sensed that something terrible was about to happen, although she could not have said what. Then things began to move very rapidly indeed.

Hearing his daughter cry out in such a piteous fashion, Moses Jackson pulled the heavy Walker from its holster and began drawing down in the general direction of the men and girls. As he did so, one of the nearby passengers, a woman of about fifty, shrieked out in alarm, 'He's got a gun, he's got a gun!'

Fearing that this signified that they were about to be robbed, murdered or who knew what all else, others took up the cry and several people got to their feet with a view to fleeing to the other end of the coach. This pandemonium suited Michel Docherty very well, for it served to distract Flynn's attention. This was not the first tight squeeze that Docherty had found himself in, not by a long chalk, and he had already decided that the smart dodge would be to abandon the girls and make a break for it. Flynn was, as he knew to his cost, like a peculiarly persistent bloodhound, and unless he could be killed would never cease in his efforts to hunt down the man he regarded with such loathing. Now that he had a line on him, Docherty had no doubt at all that Marshal Flynn would now make every effort to track him to the ends of the Earth if need be.

A stentorian roar filled the coach, quelling the hubbub, as Flynn shouted at the top of his voice, 'Get down! All you folk get down, 'less'n you want to be shot.' Whether they apprehended that he was a peace officer or were perhaps even more convinced that he was a bandit, Jed Flynn never found out, but his yelling worked the desired effect because a hush fell, and all those who had been running about like headless chickens now dropped themselves into the nearest seats in mortal fear of their lives. Just as silence descended and Flynn thought that they might yet be able to arrest the men they were after, Docherty fired twice at him. The first ball shattered the windowpane in the door through which Jackson and Flynn had entered the coach. The second found a lodging-place in the head of the old conductor, who gave a gasp of surprise and then fell dead on the floor.

The devil of it was that neither Jackson nor Flynn dared to fire towards the two men who were now both shooting in their direction for fear of hitting one of the girls. Both the former marshal and the farmer dropped out of sight behind a seat and tried to fathom out the best way of tackling the situation. While they were wondering what to do next, Docherty whispered to his partner, 'I'm going to uncouple the locomotive from the coaches. We can get away in that and leave these fools behind.' In the heat of the moment, Mortimer did not stop to consider the inherent implausibility of this scheme, and when Michael Docherty abjured him to keep the marshal and his friend occupied, he merely nodded and peered to the back of the coach, ready to fire.

It was almost too easy, and as Docherty dropped onto his hands and knees and wriggled beneath the seats, pushing aside the forest of shins that sometimes threatened to obstruct his passage to the front of the coach, he was sure that Mortimer would soon be killed, but not, he hoped, before he himself had gained the open air.

When he reached the final seat, Docherty took a chance and peeped back, just in time to see Jed Flynn standing up and evidently preparing to rush forward. He fired twice at the marshal, which caused Flynn to duck down again. As he did so, Jim Mortimer fired as well. Guessing that he would be unlikely to get a better opportunity than this, Docherty opened the door at front of the coach, slipped through and then leaped to the ground. They were making their way up a slope and so the train was moving at a little under twenty miles an hour. He rolled over and over when he landed, but as soon as he stopped he jumped to his feet. Without pausing to take breath, Docherty set off at a sprint, heading towards a group of three men who seemed to be fooling around with a bunch of long sticks and telescopes.

'This is no good,' said Flynn, as he bent down again to avoid the bullets flying towards him, 'We need to end this now or there's no telling how many innocents'll be hurt. You game to charge 'em?'

The words were hardly out of Flynn's mouth, when the other man lurched to his feet and rushed forward, giving a blood-curdling battle cry as he did so. Flynn ran forward at the same time and the two of them were upon Mortimer before he knew what was happening. Precisely as Jed Flynn had expected, as soon as they were upon the man, Jackson shot him dead, the ball burying itself in Mortimer's breast. There was no point in reproving Moses Jackson, because it was at once plain that Docherty was not there with the girls, all of who were now screaming as loud as could be. It was at this point that Flynn chanced to look out of the window and saw his quarry escaping.

The surveying team were more than a little surprised to find a man racing towards them with a gun in his hand. They were working for the railroad company and were currently measuring out a possible spur from the line running through Larkspur. None of them was armed and they stood uncertainly, waiting to see what would happen next. They were not given long to consider the matter, for Michael Docherty said breathlessly, just as soon as he was within hailing distance, 'Any man opposes me and I'll shoot him down like a dog. I'll take all those horses with me.'

'All of 'em?' exclaimed one of the party injudiciously. 'Why, you can't ride all three at once, you know.'

No sooner had he spoken than the wild-looking man coming towards them fired a shot in their general direction. The ball struck the dusty earth some ten feet from them, kicking up a shower of grit, dirt and small stones. 'Another word from any of you and I'll kill the man who speaks it.'

All three men drew the perfectly correct conclusion that this was not an instance of hyperbole and that here was a man who meant just exactly what he said. They accordingly remained silent and stood motionless beside their theodolites and measuring chains, making no attempt to interfere as Docherty freed the reins of the horses from where they had been secured to a stout post driven into the ground, and then mounted the liveliest looking beast. He then trotted away, leading the other two horses with him. His purpose was perfectly simple. He did not want that damned marshal to jump down from the train himself and then find a mount ready and waiting.

Jed Flynn tugged repeatedly on the metal handle that connected to the emergency vacuum brake. He'd little hope of catching Docherty, but if he didn't do so it would not be for want of trying. As the railroad train came to a juddering halt, almost throwing him to the floor, Jed Flynn never once took his eyes from the man he hoped to see hanged. He accordingly watched with something akin to despair as he saw Michael Docherty mount up and ride off with the only other horses in the vicinity that could be seen. There being no point in pursuing a mounted man on foot, Flynn immediately changed his plans and decided that the best move now would be to get the train to start up again and to make for Birkinville. His first duty, when all was said and done, was to see that those young girls were returned safely to their families.

After all the excitement of the last few days, it came as something of a surprise to Jedediah Flynn when he came closer to losing his life while trying to get the train to start off again than he had done since encountering the three roughnecks on the track near Harker's Crossing. He had apprehended that it would be a fairly simple and straightforward matter to leave the coach and then walk round to the cab of the locomotive and ask the driver to get moving. Leaving the coach was not hard; he left by the same door that Docherty must have used, and when he jumped down onto the sandy soil it seemed all that was needed was a courteous word or two to the driver. Walking round the tender containing the coal, Flynn was more than a little taken aback to find himself faced with a grim-faced man toting a sawn-off scattergun. This fellow, who was laying on the coal and peering down at Flynn, introduced himself by cocking his piece and saying softly, 'Don't move a muscle, as you value your life!'

Looking up slowly and being sure to keep his hands in sight and not make any sudden moves – such as might have been open to the wrong inter-pretation – Flynn saw at once that this was probably the fireman. At any rate, his visage was grimed and bedaubed with coal dust and he reeked of smoke. No doubt the recent spate of robberies on railroad trains had caused him to carry a weapon of his own, to dis-courage interference with his own train. Flynn said, 'Put up your gun. I'm a federal marshal.'

'You don't look like such,' said the man dubiously. 'You got a badge or ought of the kind?'

'There's been shooting back there. All I'm asking

is that you take this here train on to Birkinville as fast as you are able. Even if I was a bandit, which I ain't, I don't see as you could object to that. It's where you were headed anyway.'

There was a good deal of sense in what the unknown man said, and since he appeared to be unarmed and showed no signs of aggression, the stoker nodded and said, 'Well then, you get back on board and we'll be off.'

Jackson and Flynn removed the two bodies, the one being of the conductor and the other of Docherty's associate, and laid them both on the little platform outside the coach and besides the coupling. They then went to sit with the frightened and distressed girls. Jed Flynn allowed Jackson a few minutes of cuddling and reassuring his daughter while he himself spoke calmly to the other girls, including Mary Shanahan, and explained that things had changed now and that they would all be going home and not to whatever exotic destination they had previously been told. It did not escape his notice that this news was not met with cries of delight, but rather looks of dismay. Presumably, their lives were such that the prospect of visiting a few lively towns had been a more enticing one than staying home and doing the washing and cleaning.

After he felt that he had given Moses Jackson long enough for the family reunion, Flynn said to him, 'I expressly told you that I wanted no bloodshed, not unless it was needful. Do you recollect?'

Jackson looked surprised and said unapologetically, 'Fact is, I allus intended for to kill anybody I found mixed up in this business.'

'So I guessed,' replied Flynn dryly, 'but it makes it no better. Anyway, you owe me for it.'

This was perfectly acceptable to Jackson and he nodded agreeably. He had known that killing that fellow would incur some kind of penalty and he was quite ready to go to court or pay a fine or whatever else the marshal required. He knew that Flynn was the sort of man who would allow him to deliver his child safely back to his home before exacting any justice for the death of the villain who had been part of the gang.

Looking at Jackson's face, Jed Flynn read all this, and it suited his purposes very well to leave the fellow in suspense for a spell and hope that this might be punishment enough. Truth to tell, he was not himself sorry to see that man dead. Those who carried out such foul actions deserved to die, although Flynn felt that it would have been more fitting to see the man brought before a properly constituted court of law, rather than shot out of hand in that way. Still, it was done now.

At length, Jed Flynn decided that it was time to level with Jackson. Jack Brady, who looked as though he had been considerably shaken up by the recent events and was nowhere near as verbose as usual, had joined them, sitting across the aisle and looking exceedingly sober and thoughtful. Flynn said,

'You're wondering, Jackson, what I aim to do about your killing of that scallywag. Well, the answer is, nothing at all. Provided you do me a favour, that is.'

From the look in the farmer's eyes, it was clear that he had not really been anticipating a trial or anything. He and Flynn understood each other well enough, and it was quite reasonable for the marshal to ask him to do something in return for not having him indicted for homicide or something of the kind. He nodded amiably and said, 'I reckon you and me, we understand each other well enough, Marshal. What would you have of me?'

'I made a promise to Mary's mother. I swore I'd deliver her safe back to her and I wouldn't be proved false.'

Jackson cottoned on at once and said, 'You want me to take the child with me, back to Harker's Crossing? Consider it done.'

Flynn nodded in a satisfied way. Turning to the three other girls, he said, 'Where do you young ladies hail from?'

It appeared that two of them came from farms near Birkinville, and the other from a small town rather further afield. Having gained this intelligence, he said, musing out loud, 'I reckon that the police in Birkinville will take care of you three. You had a narrow escape, you know.' He outlined what he knew of life in a Mexican brothel and was pleased to note that all five girls looked a little taken aback. This was not at all what they had been led to believe. 'Mister

Brady here can give you further and fuller particulars, I believe.' For the next ten minutes, the editor of the *Clayton Counter Advertiser* regaled them with dreadful stories about girls just like themselves who had been lured into lives of unremitting degradation. It was just possible, thought Flynn, that some of this would sink in and that these silly children would think twice before waltzing off with some plausible stranger who promised them the earth.

CHAPTER 8

Jed Flynn and Moses Jackson parted when the train pulled in to Birkinville. The five girls and three men stood at the depot for a few seconds after leaving the train. There was the question of the two corpses to be delved into; the driver and stoker had both shot suspicious glances at Flynn and his companions, still not altogether sure that they were not some kind of criminals.

'You best be off, Jackson,' the former marshal said gruffly, 'else you'll be caught up in a heap of questioning and suchlike. You be sure to deliver that child back safely to her mother, now.'

'You've my word on it.' He held out his hand and the two men shook. Jackson held on to the other man's hand for a few seconds and he said, 'I'm right grateful to you, Marshal, more than you can know. Any time you're passing, be sure to come by my house and visit.'

'I reckon you done as much for me as I have for

you,' said Flynn. 'I wish you and your girl well.' Something that later struck him was that Moses Jackson had not asked why he was not himself returning to Harker's Crossing. Most likely, he had already guessed.

It was fortunate that Jackson took the advice to leave as soon as possible, because just two minutes later the stoker from the train came up with two police officers that he had found outside the depot. 'That's him,' he cried excitedly, pointing at Jed Flynn. 'He was the one as started giving the orders.'

By a stroke of ill-luck, one of the two policemen was one of those with whom Brady and Flynn had had dealings when the man had been shot and killed near the offices of the *Clayton County Advertiser*. He was not best pleased to see the two men again, especially where they were now seemingly connected with two more deaths by shooting. He said, 'Mister Brady and Marshal Flynn. I won't say as I'm pleased to see you, 'cause I'm not. What's all this about men being killed on the train you was on?'

'It's by way of being a long story . . .' began Flynn, but the two officers were not apparently in the mood for hearing any long stories.

'I'll be bound it is,' said the policeman. 'Tell you what, why don't the two of you come down to the station house and tell the captain all about it? I make no doubt that he'll be right interested to hear all about it.'

It was not the captain before whom Jack Brady and

Jed Flynn were first brought, but rather the same sergeant whom they had already met in connection with the earlier death. He looked anything but over-joyed to see them, muttering something about the 'proverbial bad penny'. Ignoring the newspaperman, he addressed Flynn, saying, 'Been getting a heap of enquiries about you. More than I care to deal with.'

'Enquiries?' asked Flynn, surprised. 'Who from?'

'Happen I'll let the captain fill you in on that. . . . Your boss wanting to know what's become of you, chiefly.'

'There's no "boss" in the case,' said Flynn irritably. 'I'm a free agent, and as soon as this business is con-cluded I'm heading north.'

This declaration was met with a sceptical and dis-believing look from the sergeant, who said, 'That ain't the impression I've been getting, but there, it's no affair of mine. Trouble follows you, Marshal Flynn, like flies 'round shit. Two more corpses you brought us, that right?'

At this moment, there came an impatient shout from an office and the sergeant hurried off to see what was wanted. He returned a few seconds later and said, 'Captain'll see you now.' Brady and Flynn both stepped forward and the policeman said, 'Not you, Brady. Just the marshal here. You just set here and don't move a muscle.'

Captain James was a plain, bluff man with no use at all for fancy words. He felt himself to be in an awkward position, and from all he understood was

141

about to become embroiled in a complicated and distasteful affair miles from the city whose peace he was sworn to uphold. He had visions of being called upon to expend large sums of money for which he would have to account to the city council at some stage. It was all a damned nuisance, and so he was utterly astonished when the man whose arrival he had been dreading said, 'Captain, you have the authority to swear me in as a peace officer, don't you?'

'Swear you in? I don't understand you, sir.'

'Once this matter of the dead men on that train is cleared up, I want you to swear me in. I've no official standing as it is. I'm no more than a private citizen.'

Remembering his manners, Captain James indicated a chair and invited his visitor to sit. Then he said slowly, 'It strikes me that you and me are speaking at cross-purposes.'

'How so?'

'I've been receiving telegrams about you since you took off with that young jackanapes, which is to say Jack Brady.'

'Telegrams? Who from?'

'Your boss. He wants to know where you've gone and to remind us that we are obliged to give you every assistance and put ourselves at your disposal.'

Now it was Jedediah Flynn's turn to feel that he and the captain were talking at cross-purposes. He said, 'There must be some error, I think. I resigned some three weeks since. I'm not a marshal anymore.'

'Then all I can think is that your people have not acted on your resignation. As far as they're concerned, you're still a United States Marshal, and if you want my help I'm duty-bound to oblige.'

Flynn rubbed his cheek meditatively. He said, half to himself, 'So the boot's all on the other foot, hey? Here I am begging you a favour and it turns out there's no need at all. Isn't that something?'

Flynn outlined the position regarding Larkspur. He had a feeling that some of what he said was already known to the police captain. When he had finished his recitation, the captain said, 'It's a filthy business and I won't pretend that I don't know something of it. These people are the devil to catch, though. Most of the girls who go off with them do so of their own volition. There's no question of them being stolen away or anything. But this is nothing to the purpose. I'm guessing that you want me to raise a party of men to go with you to Larkspur? It's what you might call a grey area, my jurisdiction that far from town, but since your boss asks it I'm willing to oblige.'

For a moment, Jed Flynn had a pleasant vision of riding back to Larkspur at the head of a posse and pictured the expressions of shock on the faces of those there who had taken him for some drifter. He smiled and said, 'It's kind of you, Captain, but it won't be needed. This is between me and Michael Docherty. I'd as soon take him down by myself. This is between him and me, you see.'

The captain understood this sentiment perfectly and was relieved that he would not, after all, be called upon to expend money and manpower in this quest. He said, 'Is there any way in which I can help?'

'Well, the fact is I only have a beat-up old cap-and-ball pistol, with neither powder nor shot to go with it. You have an arsenal or something of the sort here?'

'Sure.'

'Well then, if I could beg the loan of a rifle and pistol then I'd be eternally in your debt.'

Pleased at having got off so lightly from the whole mess, Captain James was only too happy to go along with this request. He called in the sergeant and directed that Marshal Flynn be given the run of the gunroom and allowed to take whatever weapons and ammunition he wished. As Flynn rose, he said, 'Will the men on the railroad do your bidding?'

'They generally do,' replied the captain. 'Why d'you ask?'

'I've a notion that the man I'm tracking will have taken horse and ridden hard back to Larkspur. He'll most like take what he can in cash money and portable property and then light out for a spell. If I could have somebody loan me a locomotive to race along that line without the encumbrance of coaches and so on, why then I reckon that I'd catch the fellow still in town. Course, I'd need a driver and stoker.'

'You know how to open your mouth wide,' grumbled the captain. 'Still, I'll send word down to the

depot. Easiest thing would be to uncouple the locomotive as delivered you here and turn it round in the
shunting yard. I reckon it might be done.'

Neither the stoker who had confronted Flynn with
a shotgun nor the driver of the locomotive were
enchanted to find themselves being directed to
convey him back to Larkspur. Flynn had changed
back into his own clothes and was openly carrying
both a brand new .44, which used rimfire cartridges,
and also a .56-56 carbine. The pockets of his black
jacket bulged with ammunition.

'Well, sir,' said the driver, as Flynn climbed up into
the cab of the locomotive with him, 'Captain James
has sent word to the man in charge of the depot and
he says it's to be done, but I don't mind owning that
I ain't happy 'bout it.'

'I don't all that much mind about your happiness,'
replied Flynn amicably, 'so long as you transport me
to Larkspur as fast as you're able.'

'Might not be a policeman,' muttered the man,
'but I can smell fish, alright. Yes, sir.'

Jedediah Flynn had done a lot of unusual things in
his life, more perhaps than most folk, but riding in
the cab of a railroad locomotive was a novelty for
him. The smell of the burning coal and the wind
rushing past his face was a curious combination and
he felt a boyish delight at travelling in such a way.
After attempting to start conversations with the
driver and fireman, he gave this up as a bad job, for

neither man appeared to be inclined to exchange words with him. They both clearly regarded him as a bad man who had somehow tricked the police into helping him.

The speed of the locomotive, now that it was hauling only a tender and not a line of coaches, was something remarkable, and they reached Larkspur in what seemed to the marshal to be no time at all. During the journey his wrath at the superior who had by all accounts refused to file his resignation, had abated somewhat. It had all worked out for the best in the long run, for here he was, armed and with full authority to take whatever steps he thought needful to take Michael Docherty into custody and deliver him up to justice.

Flynn had no idea how any member of the so-called 'vigilance committee' in this town would react to seeing him marching down the street with a rifle under his arm, but he was ready for anything. He was glad now that he had declined any offer of help from the Birkinville police. This was his fight and it was up to him to bring this scoundrel to justice.

As he strode down the middle of the street leading from the depot, Flynn was aware that he was garnering odd looks and enquiring glances from some of those passing along the boardwalk. Nobody challenged him, though, which was as well for all concerned. In the distance, he heard the sound of the locomotive chuffing away from the town. The men operating it had obviously decided that the sooner they were away from Larkspur, the better. All things considered, Jed Flynn could not find it in his heart to blame them.

At a guess, Docherty would at this very moment be ransacking his fine house feverishly, trying to gather together as much of his ill-gotten gains as possible, with a view to taking an extended vacation from Larkspur. He would know by now that the game was up and that justice was on his very heels. It would be a wrench to abandon the fancy lifestyle that he had created here, but when the alternative is kicking your life out at the end of a rope then anything is preferable, even a life on the run. No doubt he would suppose that Flynn would take a good length of time to gather a posse and return to Larkspur. He would hardly be expecting the marshal to be back here within a few hours.

Out of the corner of his eye, Flynn was aware of one or two men who, as soon as they caught sight of him, moved off in a determined manner, presumably to raise an alarm or notify others of his presence in town. There was little to be done about this and so he just ignored it. What he did do was keep a sharp eye on the men ahead of him, doing his best to gauge if any of them were minded to take aggressive action against him. There was staring and a distinct air of unease, but nobody did anything which might have been interpreted as hostile. Some men stopped dead in their tracks and watched him, but that was the limit of it. As he moved towards the edge of town there were fewer and fewer people about, and as far as he could see nobody made any attempt to follow him. Flynn guessed though that word was being carried to those who mattered, that he was back and on the warpath.

The weight of the carbine that he carried under his arm was comforting, as was the fact that it was cocked and ready to fire at a moment's notice. Jed Flynn was not, in the normal way of things, one for carrying loaded and primed firearms in a public place, but the circumstances were exceptional and, to his way of thinking, fully justified such a precaution.

There was no sign of anybody near or by the grand house to which he had been taken soon after fetching up in Larkspur. The wrought-iron gate still hung from the ruined gatepost, with no indication that anybody had even tried to repair it. As he approached the house, Flynn noticed that a couple of windows at the front were also broken, most likely from the blasts set off by Moses Jackson. The front door was ajar, which caused the little hairs on the back of Flynn's neck to rise; a sure and infallible sign for him that danger lurked near at hand. He brought the musket up until the butt of it was resting easily against his shoulder, although the barrel was still pointing down at the ground. Bringing it up and firing would be the work of a mere fraction of a second.

Michael Docherty was in an upstairs room, frantically throwing money and various ornaments made of silver and silver-gilt into a carpetbag. While doing so, he was also throwing documents and letters onto a fire that he had kindled in the hearth. It was a warm June day and the fire made the room unbearably hot. He had his back to Flynn, who appeared in the doorway having walked quietly up the richly carpeted stairs. When he turned and caught sight of the grim-faced marshal, with a carbine at the ready, the look of almost comical dismay upon Michael Docherty's face was a picture to behold. 'You!' he exclaimed.

'As large as life and twice as natural,' said Flynn, pleasantly. 'Going for a little trip, are you?'

'There's money here, more than you could earn in a year. It's yours for the taking.'

'There's not enough gold in the world to make me alter my plans. You ought to know that.'

'What, then?'

Flynn shook his head and said, 'You know very well what, Docherty. I'm arresting you for being a fugitive and also for the wilful murder of Timothy Grant, the guard at the penitentiary whose brains you dashed out with a rock. Remember him? His wife and little'uns have had a hard time of it since the man of the house was killed. Get your jacket.'

Docherty shook his head in amazement. He said, 'How far do you think you'll get down this road? Where you aiming to take me?'

'In the first instance, down to the railroad depot to wait for the next train west.'

'You won't get fifty yards down the road with me.'

'Well, let's give it a try.'

Jed Flynn was in no doubt that given the faintest shadow of an opportunity, Docherty would either make a run for it or, if he thought it would work better, attempt to kill the man who was now holding him at gunpoint. Flynn accordingly took great care to keep the carbine trained on his prisoner. He knew Michael Docherty to be a jackal of a man who would scruple at nothing.

The two of them walked through the shattered gateway leading to the street, with Flynn taking great care to keep a few paces behind the other man so that he would have no chance to whirl round and grab the gun. In this way they proceeded along one or two deserted streets until they reached Larkspur's main thoroughfare. Flynn knew at once, by that sixth sense that all lawmen acquire if they are spared long enough, that an ambush, trap or some other kind of unpleasant surprise had been laid for him and his captive. Pedestrians on the boardwalk halted as they passed, watching them closely as though in anticipation – although of what, Flynn did not yet know. It was not until they came within sight of the depot that he realized what was afoot.

Strung out in a straggling line across the road, blocking his path to the railroad depot, were a half dozen men. Three of them were cradling rifles and looked to Flynn to be anticipating his arrival. That trouble was imminent was suggested by the fact that although the boardwalk running alongside the stores and saloons was tolerably crowded with men who were watching the unfolding scene curiously, there were no bystanders within twenty-five yards of the group waiting for him and his prisoner. Those living in or visiting Larkspur often guessed when violence was about to erupt, and unless they were actively involved in the cause of the quarrel took good care not to put themselves in hazard.

Up until this point, Michael Docherty had been trudging down the middle of the street with a faintly hangdog air. He was aware of the great fall from being 'the boss' one minute and the next finding himself marched along at gunpoint. At the sight of the armed gang standing in the roadway and guarding the approach to the depot, he seemed to grow jaunty. Turning to Flynn with a smirk on his face, he said cockily, 'What did I tell you, you bastard? You're not going to be taking me anywhere.'

'Well, let's see how things pan out.' replied the other, not slowing down or giving any outward sign of perturbation. 'We'll see what these boys want. They're after a fight, I can oblige them.'

'Why, you damned fool, they outnumber you seven to one! You think you can take them all on and win? I don't think it for a moment.'

Although he wasn't about to own it to his prisoner, Jed Flynn was forced to admit to himself that Docherty had a very sound point. The men ahead were strung out like a picket line, making it plain that they were there to inhibit free passage of the road to the depot. The three men holding rifles looked to Flynn's eyes as though they knew how to handle them. Of the remaining four, three looked like tough types, with pistols at their hips. The fourth was a harder study: a man of about Flynn's own age, very smartly dressed. He looked more like a bank manager than anything else and was possessed of an indefinable air of authority. Flynn guessed that he was in some way in charge of the other men.

Jedediah Flynn was not in the habit of allowing other men to impose their will upon him, and so as he drew nigh to the body of armed men he decided that whatever else happened, Michael Docherty would not be walking free that day. The carbine was cocked and pointing straight at Docherty's spine. If anybody were foolish enough to fire on Flynn, then it would be the work of a moment to squeeze the trigger and deliver justice to the white slaver. Of course, he himself would then be as good as dead, but that could not be helped. He could see no conceivable way that events this day were going to turn out in his favour. All that remained was to order his death in the most fitting way that could be managed.

When Flynn and Docherty were thirty feet or so from the men standing in their way, Flynn halted and said to his prisoner, 'Just hold up now. You stand still and don't move so much as your eyebrows, 'less'n you want me to shoot you down like the mangy cur that you are.' Having delivered himself of these views, he reached slowly down and drew with his left hand the pistol that he had been loaned by the police at Birkinville. He did not aim it particularly at any of the men ahead of him, but wanted to know that when the shooting started, he was good and ready. As he took the pistol from where it nestled in the holster, Flynn lowered the butt of his musket so that it was resting comfortably on his right hip, although still pointing at Docherty. As he made his preparations, Flynn suddenly recollected himself and realized that so busy had he been with the calculating the logistics of killing that he had quite forgot to ready himself for facing the Lord.

'Lord, I hope you'll receive my soul, should I not make it through this here,' Flynn muttered quietly. 'Amen.'

'What's that you say, you pious son of a bitch?' enquired Docherty.

'Hush your mouth now,' directed Flynn, for it was certain-sure that a stroke of lightning would soon fall upon at least one or two of those present in that street, which was a fearful thing to consider.

There was a tense silence, which anybody could have predicted would in the end be broken by the sound of gunfire. So it proved, but not in the way that any observer who knew nothing of the background to the confrontation could possibly have foreseen. Neither Flynn nor the men facing him had spoken. He and the gang of what he guessed to be members of Larkspur's vigilance committee just stared at each other, waiting. When the shot came, expected as it was, Jed Flynn started in surprise, because none of the men he was watching so narrowly had made any move. The sound came instead from some good distance away and behind Flynn. As he whirled round to meet what he apprehended was an enemy behind him, he saw that the shot had not been aimed at him or, if it had, it had gone astray. The back of Michael Docherty's head was all over blood and, as Flynn watched, the former 'boss' of the town dropped to the ground in front of him.

There was no way of telling where the shot that had killed Docherty had come from; Flynn's best guess was from a rooftop or window down the street a-ways. He turned back to the men, whom he had supposed to be menacing him, and saw to his astonishment that they had relaxed and were now standing easy. Before he could fathom out what to make of this, the well-dressed man said, 'Lord a-mercy, what a terrible thing to happen. Two of you go up the street there and see if you can find who shot that poor man.' With barely disguised smiles, as though this was a great joke, two of the men with rifles sauntered off up the street. They were obviously not in a hurry and Flynn could see that this was no more than a piece of play-acting.

'You must be Marshal Flynn,' said the fellow who was apparently in charge of matters. 'I brought some of our vigilance men down here to aid you taking that villain off to meet his just desserts. Looks like we weren't needed, though. Still, we can lend you a hand in taking the corpse to the depot.'

In a flash, the whole thing was laid bare to Jed Flynn and he cursed himself for a simpleton. For all that he might have helped establish Larkspur as a profitable venture, Michael Docherty, once he had been identified by a federal marshal as a wanted killer, had become a liability to his erstwhile business partners and they wanted to be rid of him. They would also increase their own wealth in the process, of course. Flynn himself had never been in danger today and those men had not been waiting there to attack or even threaten him. Their whole entire purpose had been to get him and Docherty to stand still so that one of their friends up on a rooftop could get a clear shot, taking Michael Docherty out of the equation for good and all. Presumably, the others who had been running the town with him would now be a good deal richer, having inherited all Docherty's share in the various rackets that had made this little place such a goldmine.

'This isn't ended,' growled Flynn. 'I'll be coming back with more men and then we'll see what's what.'

'You'll be more than welcome, Marshal,' said the man who was probably one of the new 'bosses'. 'I was sorely deceived by that scoundrel. Had I known he was wanted by the law, why, I would have turned him in at once.' There were a few chuckles at this from the men standing around, who seemed to find it good sport to see a marshal bated in this fashion.

155

At a guess, just as soon as he had left town, this odious fellow and his gang would set to and destroy any incriminating evidence upon which they could lay their hands. Doubtless some of the girls would be sent away from the hurdy houses, and by the time Flynn returned with reinforcements everything would be as clean as could be. Anything at all shady would be blamed on the man whom he had just seen shot down in front of him. Truly, there was no honour among thieves, and it was altogether possible that plans had already been in hand to dispose of Docherty and seize his wealth before Flynn had turned up here. Perhaps his arrival merely acted as a catalyst or trigger for something that would have happened in any case.

Walking up right close to the man who now fancied himself the new leader of this community, Flynn said softly, 'My name is Marshal Jedediah Flynn. I promise you now that I will be back here before too long, and however you try and cover your misdeeds I will find out enough to see you behind bars. You think I believe that this filthy trade in young women was all Docherty's doing, without any aid from others? Your hands are dirty too, mister, and I'll make it my life's work to see justice done upon you.'

The man to whom he was speaking shrugged, reached into his jacket and extracted a slim cigar, which he proceeded to light. After blowing out a stream of fragrant smoke, he smiled broadly and said, 'I wish you luck with your venture, Marshal. We'll be sure to have a good welcome awaiting you and your friends.'

There was little point in standing and bandying words with such a skunk, and Flynn said nothing, but walked right past the man and headed to the depot. Two of the vigilance men had carried the body of the late Michael Docherty to the side of the tracks, and when Flynn got there one of them asked, 'Where d'you want us to leave him, Marshal?' Flynn stared at these two, as though trying to impress their features upon his memory so that he would later be able to identify them. When they saw that he was not minded to answer them, the men pitched the corpse of their one-time boss in the dust and walked off, back towards Main Street.

By a mercy, Jed Flynn only had to wait a little less than an hour for the next train heading towards Birkinville. The conductor was none too pleased to find his train being used to transport a dead body, but the marshal was most insistent and quoted very statutes that touched upon the fearsome penalties for obstructing a federal peace officer in the execution of his duties.

As the railroad train clattered and rocked its way west, Flynn wondered idly what the police in Birkinville would say when he turned up with yet another corpse. Well, he could hardly have left the body behind. This was, after all, a wanted man. He fell to planning the best means of raising a posse and undertaking a raid on Larkspur. It would not be something that could be arranged in a hurry, and he was very much afraid that he would have to delay his enrolment at the theological college. After all, there were many ways of doing the Lord's work and maybe tracking down the ungodly and bringing them to judgement was as worthy as preaching from a pulpit. He would have to see.

CHAPTER 9

US Marshal Jedediah Flynn
Eastern District of Kansas
222 W. Avenue
Topeka
7th July 1872

The Northern Baptist Seminary
132 Glover Road
Lafayette
Illinois

Sir,

    I regret that I am compelled to inform you that I shall no longer be able to take up the place at your college, where I was due to begin studying for the Ministry this coming fall. Circumstances have conspired to keep me in my present line of work for at least another six months and I shall accordingly be detained beyond the commencement of term in September. This is a matter of considerable regret to me and

I hope that you are not put to any inconvenience as a consequence.

God willing, I shall have cleared up all further outstanding professional matters within three months or so, and wonder if it would be possible to postpone my enrolment until next September. I am confident that by then, I shall be able to resign from my position and therefore be free to devote all my attention to studying for this new career, to which I feel called.

I remain, sir, your obedient servant,
Jedediah Flynn (US Marshal).